The Cygnus Constellation

The Cygnus Constellation

Yolande Villemaire

translated by Margaret Wilson Fuller

Ekstasis  Editions

The original edition of this book, *La constellation du cygne*, was published by TYPO in 1996.

Published in 2017 by:
Ekstasis Editions Canada Ltd.   Ekstasis Editions
Box 8474, Main Postal Outlet   Box 571
Victoria, BC V8W 3S1   Banff, AB T1L 1E3

LIBRARY AND ARCHIVES CANADA CATALOGUING IN PUBLICATION

Villemaire, Yolande
[Constellation du cygne. English]
  The Cygnus constellation / Yolande Villemaire ; translated by Margaret Wilson Fuller.

Translation of: La constellation du cygne.
Issued in print and electronic formats.
ISBN 978-1-77171-145-6 (paperback).--ISBN 978-1-77171-146-3 (ebook)

  I. Fuller, Margaret Wilson, translator II. Title. III. Title: Constellation du cygne. English.

PS8593.I39C6513 2017   C843'.54   C2015-907819-9
                    C2015-907820-2

Canada Council Conseil des Arts Canadä
for the Arts du Canada

Ekstasis Editions acknowledges financial support for the publication of *The Cygnus Constellation* from the government of Canada through the Canada Book Fund and the Canada Council for the Arts, and from the Province of British Columbia through the Book Publishing Tax Credit. We acknowledge the financial support of the Government of Canada through the National Translation Program for Book Publishing, an initiative of the *Roadmap for Canada's Official Languages 2013-2018: Education, Immigration, Communities*, for our translation activities.

Printed and bound in Canada

"... Everything that can be said can be said clearly;
What we cannot speak about we must pass over in silence"

~ Ludwig Wittgenstein

The Cygnus Constellation

Celia Rosenberg

Paris, August 15, 1940. The sky is grey. Celia Rosenberg's gaze follows the pigeons as they scatter at her feet and fly away. The man beside her walks with a heavy tread. She can feel him looming over her on her left. She holds a cigarette in her left hand. A gitane *maïs* stained with her orange lipstick. She raises it to her lips. Blows the smoke out towards the grey clouds scudding above their heads. Into the damp air.

The man's footsteps ring out on the deserted Paris sidewalk. It can't be six o'clock yet. Celia Rosenberg is walking in the grey desert of Paris. Following in her wake, the last of the night's customers. Grey Paris pigeon. Paris, grey pigeon. Last pigeon of the night.

She turns her head slightly to the left, looks at him. He is looking straight ahead, his mind elsewhere. He will not be her first German soldier. At least they don't talk. Or, if they do, she doesn't have to pretend to listen to them. Celia Rosenberg takes another drag on her cigarette. She looks at him again. Fair-hair, pink complexion, well scrubbed. The word "syphilis" gnaws at her gut as she walks on her black, high-heeled crocodile-skin shoes along Boulevard Haussmann, Paris, August 15. Paris, grey pigeon.

Taking another drag on her gitane she expels her anxiety. and the grey smoke curls above her black-clad figure, her voluptuous breasts, eyes dark as coals, orange mouth.

Arriving in front of her building, she slows down, stops and, with the toe of her elegant shoe, puts out the cigarette which is beginning to burn her fingers. The man has stopped, he is standing beside her, massive, silent, somber. She looks at him. For an instant their eyes meet. He seems weary, exhausted. It is hot in spite of the early hour. Celia Rosenberg thrusts her hand into her bag, rummages in it for several long minutes before finding the key to her ground floor apartment. She opens the door, forces what she hopes is a smile, motions to the man to enter. He bends his head slightly, although he doesn't need to, and enters the apartment.

It is dark. After closing the door behind her Celia Rosenberg crosses the two rooms, and lights a small lamp with a cream lampshade which casts a soft shadow on the bed. The heavy velvet drapes are closed. The heat is suffocating.

The soldier has sat down on a big armchair that takes up the narrow space between the bed and the window. He has loosened his collar. He is massaging his neck, his features are drawn, he looks immensely weary. Celia Rosenberg takes another cigarette from her gold plated case, offers him one. He accepts. She looks for a light. He takes a lighter out of his pocket, lights it. She takes the lighter from him, studies it. It is gold plated. He motions that it is a gift. She smiles, places the lighter on the small lace covered table beside her. They smoke in silence. She, standing in her black high heels in front of the thick velvet drapes. He, sitting, bareheaded, his officer's cap on his knees. She sighs.

She excuses herself, disappears behind the lacquered screen. She takes off her shoes, keeps her black silk stockings on and slips her slim, high-arched feet into orange-coloured poult-de-soie pumps. Peels off her dress in a single movement. She is wearing a lace slip which she also takes off. Her delicate black lace bra, panties and garter belt emphasize Celia Rosenberg's milky white stomach, arms and thighs. She puts on a flesh coloured slip over her underwear which shows through the delicate silk. She folds the screen, leaving her wrinkled black dress and slip on it. She walks towards the soldier who is watching her with an amused expression. Picks up the cigarette burning in the copper ashtray on the small table. As she bends over in front of him, the man catches a glimpse of her breasts spilling out of her slip. He mutters something. She smiles at him. Moves closer. Offers him her breasts. He buries his blonde head in them. She smells musk, cigarettes, sweat and sex. He seizes her round the waist so violently that she gives a small cry of pain and surprise. She is suddenly a little frightened by the violence of the man's desire. She extricates herself, backs off a few steps, studies him. The soldier's face and neck are flushed with a kind of stubborn passion. Disconcerted, he looks at her. She enjoys this immobility. She lets him look.

Now he is smiling at her. Confident. He is waiting. Keeping her gaze on him, she stubs out her cigarette. Kneels in front of him. Slowly, she undoes his fly, her grey eyes gazing deep into the German soldier's green eyes. He is still smiling. She frees the man's organ from the rough cloth trousers. His penis is long, thick, swollen with desire. She holds it for a moment between her fingers. The tip stands out clearly, protuberant, rimmed by a fold of pink flesh. She brings her mouth closer. The man moans. She brushes his penis gently with her lips. It is very hot, very quiet in Celia Rosenberg's room. She engulfs the tip with her mouth, then, slowly, sliding her lips around the shaft, she draws half the penis into her mouth. The man tastes of salt and urine. Then, oddly, of grass. Lost in concentration, Celia Rosenberg glides her orange mouth around the German soldier's increasingly engorged penis. He has put his big hand on Celia Rosenberg's black hair. She shivers slightly as she sucks him assiduously.

The man sighs, his breath comes more quickly, he cries out, moves his pelvis as Celia Rosenberg sucks his swollen penis till it explodes in her mouth. She laps up the sperm, licks the German soldier's organ meticulously. His eyes are closed. A vague smile hovers on his lips. "You would think he were dead," Celia thinks. She gets up. Adjusts the bodice of her slip, reaches for her cigarette case. He intercepts her hand, raises it to his lips, smiles at her. She returns his smile.

The soldier straightens his clothes, digs in his trouser pocket. He pulls out a thousand franc bill, lays it on the small table. She picks up the bill, places it in the drawer of the dark wood night table. Celia Rosenberg goes over to the wardrobe on the far wall of the apartment. She rummages among the hangers, takes down a coral-coloured peignoir. White swans glide gracefully along the sleeves and around the collar. Celia Rosenberg drapes herself in it, ties a white cord around her waist. She looks at herself in a big cheval mirror and, fingers curved, fluffs out her fine dark hair. Shakes her head.

The soldier says something in German. She turns round, looks at him. He waves another thousand franc bill, lays it on the small table, smiles. She shakes her head. He says something else in German. Softly, almost sadly. She shakes her head, signals no with her hands. He smiles, says "Oui?", digs in his pocket, extracts another thousand franc bill, unfolds it and holds it out to her. He looks into her eyes beseechingly, but with a touch of irony. He speaks to her, almost in a whisper, in German. Celia Rosenberg doesn't understand what he is saying. He repeats, "Oui?", holds the bill out to her again. She doesn't take it. She doesn't speak. She remains standing in front of the seated man. She doesn't speak. He places the thousand franc bill beside the other one on the small table. She doesn't react. He stands up, picks up the two bills. Celia Rosenberg sits down on the edge of the bed. She is tired, very tired. Again he says something in German. She looks at him. He opens the night table drawer, throws the two bills into it, closes the drawer. He bends towards her, looks into her eyes. She shakes her head gently, no. He places his lips on hers, kisses her. Automatically, she kisses him back. He slides a hand inside the neckline of her peignoir, puts his arm around her waist. The warmth of the embrace surprises Celia Rosenberg.

She gives in indifferently. The man pushes her down onto the bed. He buries his blonde head between Celia Rosenberg's breasts, frees them from the bra which is stretched tight beneath her slip, licks her right breast. Clasps her to him. She abandons herself to his warmth. Carefully, he slides the slip over her head, removes her panties and bra. Celia Rosenberg is now wearing only her black lace garter belt and black silk stockings. He takes her breasts between his hands, kneads them, kisses them. She closes her eyes. He kisses her belly button, travels down to her vulva, places his lips on her moist labia. It is very hot in Celia Rosenberg's bedroom. The German soldier opens Celia Rosenberg's labia with his tongue, circles her clitoris, caresses the mouth of her vagina. Eyes closed, she surrenders. She is breathing slowly, as if in a trance.

Suddenly, he grasps her buttocks hard, moves his mouth vigorously between Celia Rosenberg's unresisting thighs. The stubble on his cheek is prickly. With a violent thrust of her hips, Celia Rosenberg frees herself. Her grey eyes blaze with fury as she grabs her peignoir with one hand, covers herself irritably, sits on the edge of the bed, gets up. Still half lying on the bed which she has just left so abruptly, he watches her in astonishment.

The man strokes his rough cheek thoughtfully. Celia Rosenberg is standing in front of the window. She opens the heavy drapes slightly letting the sombre grey morning light filter into the apartment. She lets the drapes fall back into place, takes a cigarette out of her gold-plated cigarette case. The German soldier has sat up in the bed. He has taken off his boots. Watches her. Speaks to her in German. She doesn't understand German.

He talks for a long time, indifferent to her silence. She simply looks at him. He has taken off his jacket, rolled up his shirt sleeves. It is very hot in Celia Rosenberg's bedroom. She stands, smoking beside the small lace covered table between the window and the bed. He talks on and on. She wonders what he is talking about. From time to time, he smiles at her. Celia Rosenberg is tired, very tired.

Suddenly, he gets up, seizes Celia Rosenberg around the waist and thrusts her onto the bed. She struggles, tries to get up, but he looks straight into her eyes, says a few words in an icy tone. She closes her eyes. He kisses her eyelids. Now he is speaking softly, very softly. He repeats the same word several times. She opens her eyes. He kisses her on the mouth, clasps her to him, loosens her peignoir from her shoulders, parts her legs. She watches him. He is holding his penis in his hand so he can penetrate her more easily, plunges into her. She feels the weight of his hard organ, its thickness between her thighs. She waits. He penetrates her with a slow, continuous movement. He doesn't have an orgasm yet. She moans beneath him, moves her hips. He is still moving slowly, holding her in his arms, his nose and mouth buried in her left shoulder.

Celia Rosenberg suddenly wants to weep. This man, who is taking her with such intensity, moves her deeply. He gives a low moan, pulls out slightly, kisses her, looks into her eyes, thrusts into her again. His erection grows, his desire radiates through Celia Rosenberg's vagina, luminous needles stream from her body as it becomes lighter and lighter beneath his embrace. This man who doesn't come disturbs her. Bedazzled, she floats on waves of gold and jade. But she desperately wants him to come, please let him come.

He murmurs something in German. She doesn't understand German. He whispers softly in her ear. His voice, his breath, his belly are warm. It is very hot in Celia Rosenberg's bedroom. Celia Rosenberg has tears in her eyes. The man looks at her, smiles at her. She smiles back, sighs.

She weeps as the man penetrates her more and more gently, until she is no more than a trembling abandoned mass in the arms of the German soldier who is moaning softly against her ear and licking it from time to time. Celia Rosenberg weeps in the arms of a man whom she does not know and who is taking her as no one has ever taken her before.

Coming back to her senses, she moves her pelvis convulsively, thrashes her arms and legs about, shakes with the spasms of a simulated orgasm intended to make him come. But the man smiles and continues on his wave of pleasure without abandoning himself to it. He thrusts his increasingly hard organ rhythmically into Celia Rosenberg's moist vagina. She feels waves of orange heat penetrate to her depths, forcing involuntary small cries from her. Her pelvis dances beneath the man's, her entire body is trembling, her cries are so shrill that she eventually becomes aware of them and makes an effort to silence them while every cell in her body is spiralling up in a great wind, propelling her into visions of nebula. The man cries out, his breath comes faster. Celia Rosenberg tries to catch her breath as the rhythm of their joining increases imperceptibly until they are both carried away wildly on a tidal wave, then fall back, heavy yet floating in each other's arms. They fall asleep half clad, tangled in Celia Rosenberg's peignoir and the German soldier's trousers which have wound around his ankles. Celia Rosenberg's room is stiflingly hot.

She dreams she is climbing the statue of a black lion. It is a huge lion, big as a mountain, big as a castle. A black stone lion. It looks as if it is made of burnt wood. It is very steep. She stops on a ledge near a crevice filled with swirling white water. White foam hangs in the air along its walls. She continues climbing towards the black lion's head. But it is covered in mold. In a round pool she catches sight of a green-skinned magician who sticks out a thick tongue and rolls her eyes.

She is wakened by loud snoring. The German soldier is asleep on his back, his mouth wide open. She wants to get up, tell him to leave. But she drifts with the sensation of being on her back, in her bed, flying over Paris. She flies, feet first, passes the Eiffel Tower, turns her head carefully so as not to overbalance, looks at the Eiffel Tower covered with a sort of climbing plant, wonders whether she has only her sheet beneath her or her whole bed. But, before discovering the answer to her question, Celia Rosenberg slips into the shadows of a dreamless sleep.

The bells of Saint Augustin strike noon. Then one o'clock, then two. The heat in Celia Rosenberg's bedroom is more and more stifling. Gradually, she emerges into consciousness. First a feeling of well-being, of languid happiness rises to the surface. Then Celia Rosenberg remembers how, as she fell asleep, she could feel their mingled juices leaking from her and, with a half conscious wave of desire, she slides her body against the man's back, curling up against his warmth and sweat. She falls asleep again only to emerge a few minutes later, burning with desire.

Celia Rosenberg is now completely awake. She raises herself on her elbow, studies the German soldier's back. It is muscular but the skin is as soft as a baby's. Very pink in the dim grey light filtering through the drapes. Celia Rosenberg looks at the man's back, his shoulders, his very short blonde hair. She also takes in his waist, his buttocks, thighs and legs. She doesn't touch any part of his body, but the memory of this body arouses a sort of animal fever in her. To her great displeasure, Celia Rosenberg realizes that she wants this man.

As if in answer to this desire, the man turns over in his sleep. She nestles against the golden hairs of his chest. He embraces her, rolls gently from one side to the other with his burden in his arms, seeks Celia Rosenberg's lips, kisses her passionately. She enjoys the kiss which continues until she has an orgasm. Her eyes glisten with tears. The man gazes at her. She looks at him. They smile at each other.

The man bursts out laughing. He disentangles himself from the trousers bunched round his ankles, pulls off his socks, takes Celia Rosenberg in his arms and picks her up. She struggles, laughing. He sets her down on the armchair, pulls back the chenille bedspread and sprawls out on the cool sheets with a sigh of pleasure. It is stiflingly hot in Celia Rosenberg's room. He says something to her in German. She doesn't understand German. But she understands what he has said. She sees the German soldier's erect penis and her need for this man is so great that it is painful. Celia Rosenberg does not understand what is happening.

But she plays the game. Seductively, she lets her crumpled peignoir slide down, bares her shoulders. The German soldier whistles admiringly. She throws him a furious look. He covers his mouth with his hand like a child who has just been up to mischief. She lets the silk peignoir slide down to her feet, unfastens her stockings, rolls them down, slowly, provocatively. The man's expression is now serious as he watches her. He holds his penis in his right hand and masturbates dreamily as she removes her garter belt and crosses to the bed. He pulls her onto him, penetrates her violently. She rides him fervently, carried away, set ablaze by the white light of the fire that is consuming her, their bodies merged in a sort of electric storm. Celia Rosenberg gallops from orgasm to orgasm, floods the man as he ejaculates crying, collapses in a state of total bliss. Four o'clock strikes. The four strokes resonate deep inside Celia Rosenberg. She is bathed in sweat. Time stands still. The man beneath her is still trembling violently. They drift in space.

Celia Rosenberg smiles in her sleep, screws up her eyes to protect herself from the sun shining through the trembling foliage of the magnolias in her dream. The rustling of leaves echoes in her head as she turns it to the side. She opens her eyes on the leaden grey light creeping into her bedroom. Paris seems white hot: Paris is no more than a thin shaft of light between two rose velvet drapes in Celia Rosenberg's bedroom.

The soldier's boots, carefully lined up beside the bed, catch her eye. Celia Rosenberg gets up, slips her feet into the boots that are much too big for her. She likes the feel of the cool leather on her bare legs. She picks up the officer's cap and jacket. She studies herself in this disguise in the big mirror beside the bathroom. The German soldier's seed flows from her vagina, trickles down her shapely thighs. She stands straight, head held high, legs apart, feet firmly planted on the coffee-coloured carpet.

A knot forms in her stomach, spreads uncomfortable tension throughout her body. She takes off the cap, jacket and boots. The bells of St Augustin strike five. She goes into the bathroom, switches on the light and turns on the hot water tap. The bathtub fills with boiling water. Through the half open door, Celia Rosenberg observes the motionless shape of the German soldier beneath the white sheet. Steam rises in the already oppressively humid air, forming a screen so that the bed is lost in the white gloom. "You would think he were dead," Celia thinks. She turns off the hot water tap and turns on the cold one. There is a clap of thunder in the distance. Celia Rosenberg plunges her sweating body into the scalding bathwater.

While she is soaking in the hot, oppressive silence of her bathroom, a thunderstorm breaks. She hears the thunder claps coming closer and closer together, listens to the rain beating down. She closes her eyes and relishes the moment. Celia Rosenberg feels relieved that torrential rain is finally breaking up this stifling day. She is sweating profusely, streaming with salt sweat. She realizes she is crying for no reason. From relief perhaps. She gets out of the bath tub, and dries herself gently.

It is much cooler in the bedroom now. Celia Rosenberg goes to the wardrobe, chooses a dress, a slip and underwear. She picks up the officer's cap, jacket and boots. She walks towards the bed. The sun has just appeared behind the drapes. Celia Rosenberg hides behind one of the velvet drapes, pulls the other aside. The sun, dazzling in the grey gloom of the Paris sky, sweeps into Celia Rosenberg's bedroom and casts its light on the bed where the German soldier is still sleeping, blonde and pink in the snow white sheets.

Celia Rosenberg closes the curtain, sits down on the edge of the bed intending to wake her client. The man is sleeping peacefully, his features relaxed. He has a heavy beard. She thinks that he will want to shave. She changes her mind, doesn't wake him. She feels a vague desire growing deep within her. She gets up quickly, withdraws behind the Chinese lacquered screen. She puts on a black silk bra, silk stockings that she attaches to elastic garters decorated with white ribbons. She slips into black silk panties and a black lace slip. She goes over to the night table, picks up a bottle of perfume, puts a few drops in the hollow of her elbows and neck, goes back behind the screen to slip on her delicate crocodile pumps.

The lemony scent of the vetiver perfume fills her with joy as she arranges a silk flower in her hair. Then she puts on the dress she has decided to wear today. While she is admiring the rainbow design against a raised background of blue-black clouds decorating the Chinese screen, Celia Rosenberg suddenly remembers that it is wartime. But all her twenty-year-old body feels is love. As if life were this velvety plenitude flowing through her veins as she folds the screen, certain that the war will not last. Certain that the war is ending.

The soldier is still sleeping peacefully in the room that is growing darker. Celia Rosenberg goes into her bathroom again, turns on the light, and searches for mascara in her make up bag. She powders the tip of her nose, carefully outlines her eyes. While she is applying mascara to her long eyelashes with a little brush, Celia Rosenberg thinks she catches a glimpse of the green magician sticking her tongue out at her in the mirror. But the image evaporates as quickly as it appeared.

It is now almost dark in Celia Rosenberg's room. She opens her cigarette case, takes one out, lights it with the lighter that the soldier has given her and settles herself comfortably in the big armchair beside the bed. She smokes quietly as the night shadows steal slowly into the bedroom. The soldier is still sleeping so peacefully that she can't even hear him breathing. "You would think he were dead," Celia thinks. It is comfortable in the room now. The storm has cooled the air. Celia Rosenberg smokes in silence in her bedroom which is now completely dark. She gropes for the shell on the small lace covered table. She stubs her cigarette out on the ashtray, holds the conch to her ear. From the depths of the shell she hears the distant murmur of waves. She sees herself again, a little girl in a white dress running along the beach, the wind sighing around her. She sees herself again running against the sea spray shouting, "Julian, Julian, wait for me!"

Her heart aches at the thought of Julian. Celia Rosenberg replaces the shell, stretches voluptuously. She gets up. Turns on the little lamp with the cream shade and discovers that the bulb has blown. So she turns on the ceiling lamp. The bedroom is now bathed in a rather harsh amber light. The man groans, buries his head under the sheet.

When he opens his eyes, Celia Rosenberg is peeling an orange and laying the peel on the night table. She separates the segments and hands him one with a smile. He sits up on the bed, takes the segment, swallows it with relish. She laughs. Hands him another piece. He swallows it just as greedily. Celia Rosenberg peels another orange segment, skins it and raises the flesh to her mouth. She gives him another piece of orange. He copies her, taking the skin off the flesh before wolfing it down. They laugh. The bells of St Augustin strike six. Celia Rosenberg puts a finger to her lips to silence the German soldier so that he can count the strokes. She holds up her left hand, fingers outstretched, counts on them. Then she shows the other hand with just one finger held up. The soldier understands that it is six o'clock. He says "Ja". Jumps out of bed, parts the drapes. Paris is very grey again. But darkness has not fallen yet. Only in Celia Rosenberg's room, behind the heavy velvet drapes is it already night. The man has just turned off the light. He is whistling in the dark. He does not move. Celia Rosenberg is suddenly overcome by fear. She feels trapped, unable to make a single movement, unable to breathe. She waits, frozen to the spot. The German soldier is still whistling.

She can feel him coming towards her in the dark. But, petrified, she still does not move. He is whistling against her neck now, saying something in German, his voice a question mark, not at all a threat. Celia Rosenberg bursts into tears when he takes her in his arms.

He pretends to bite her ear, makes animal noises, a lion, an elephant, a monkey. Celia Rosenberg is now convulsed with laughter, pretends to scratch him, meowing like a panther. They struggle silently for a moment. Then, with a great roar, the man throws Celia Rosenberg, who is shaking with laughter, onto the floor. He pins her beneath him, her back pressed hard against the carpet. She freezes. He loosens his grip, she frees herself. He catches her, turns her on her stomach, lifts up her dress, tears off her panties and penetrates her suddenly from behind. Celia Rosenberg, on all fours, is still laughing. But soon she stops laughing. The man is penetrating her violently. He is speaking German. He is shouting. Celia Rosenberg takes fright. She says, "Stop". He stops. Bends over her neck, kisses her neck, caresses her breasts. Strokes her clitoris gently with his finger. Slowly slides his penis into her vagina. It becomes more engorged, stops moving. He comes without a sound and collapses onto Celia Rosenberg's back as she sinks into the coffee-coloured carpet.

He raises himself, turns her over gently, and, with deft strokes of his tongue on her vulva, brings her to orgasm with his mouth. She tries to free herself but he stops her, applies his mouth to her vulva again. She explodes again as the German soldier drinks her juices and brings her to orgasm once more. Celia Rosenberg, watches the wind stir the pink flowers of a hypnotic magnolia and bathes in its sweet scent. The German soldier has laid his head on her belly. He lets it lull him.

Celia Rosenberg feels lost, completely lost. She is quiet now that the image of magnolias is fading into the distance of her daydream. She likes the weight of the German soldier's head on her belly. She likes his silence, how his head, abandoned to the rhythm of her breath, rises and falls in tune with it.

They remain like this for several long minutes, quiet, in the dark. Their skins, their senses, their souls speak to each other. They don't say anything. They are quiet. The bells of Saint Augustin strike seven. They don't move. They stay there, motionless, wide awake, eyes closed, silent. Aware of the presence of the other, their breath, their warmth. Clinging to this instant. Motionless in this instant. Eternal.

The bells fall silent. Celia Rosenberg sees the magnolias again, the breeze that makes them tremble, the blue valley. She shifts in her dream, pulls the warm shape of the German soldier onto her belly. The are making love beneath a magnolia in a garden in Louisiana. The sky is blue, there is a gentle breeze. The hummingbirds are singing in the treetops. The grass smells good, the sun is warm.

The man bites Celia Rosenberg's belly. She opens her eyes, takes his head in her hands, kisses him on the mouth. Then, still holding his head in her hands, she gazes at him. Celia Rosenberg's eyes are shining, black diamonds in the shadowy light. The man strokes her back lightly. Perhaps they will never see each other again. This thought haunts them while their bodies are still quivering with pleasure, with the strong physical attraction between them.

Celia Rosenberg is still holding the German soldier's head. Again, she brings her lips close to his, blows into his mouth. Sitting on Celia Rosenberg's bedroom floor they mingle their breath, silently, solemnly. They remain like this for a long time, suspended on the rhythmic pattern of their perfectly attuned breath..

The man picks Celia Rosenberg up very slowly, lays her on the bed, very slowly takes off her dress and underwear. She lets him do as he wishes, attentive to his every movement. She opens her arms, pulls him to her. Again she blows in his mouth; he responds. Their bodies merge in a luminous white heat that emanates from them, a living membrane within which they move slowly.

The man has imperceptibly slid his penis into Celia Rosenberg's vagina. Their bodies tremble, united on a joyous wave. They rise and fall on a sea of vibrations which follows the rhythm of their breath, brings them closer and closer. They are both weeping, mingling their tears, swallowing each other's salt and saliva. The ocean of sensations swells, rising and falling from the crest of a tidal wave breaking in their organs, in their heads. Celia Rosenberg pictures winged seahorses. The man suddenly arches his arms and legs, raises his head. Celia Rosenberg has the impression of being penetrated by a bird. The man spreads himself over her like a swan, its white wings quivering, a wave cresting on a wave. Celia Rosenberg breathes deeply in a rustling of wings.

The man is now massaging her shoulders and shoulder blades, his fingers going deep into the flesh. She clings to his neck, tips her head back. Ten, twenty, thirty, forty, a hundred, a thousand, ten thousand suns explode behind her eyelids. Celia

Rosenberg, dazzled, shaken by spasms, convulses beneath the man whose body takes on the moving shape of her body and trembles in tune with hers. She raises her head, he finds her mouth again, blows into her mouth.

Celia Rosenberg lets go, abandons herself completely to the rising tide of molten gold that is setting her on fire. She gives in to the fissure opening within her, a blue crevasse in which she spins, a mother-of-pearl nautilus, a pearl-woman, revealed in the oyster. The German soldier floats with her on the distant high seas, blows in her mouth. Love steals in. Celia Rosenberg knows that she wants this man.

Karl-Heinz Hausen

Paris, August 16, 1940. Paris, grey pigeon. Celia Rosenberg and Karl-Heinz Hausen are walking in the gardens of the Louvre. It is cold, the sky is grey. Celia Rosenberg is wearing a grey hat, a grey costume, grey shoes and gloves. She is very pale. Karl-Heinz Hausen, his hand on the back of her neck, is solemn. The museum attendant gives them a hateful look as they enter the Egyptian Antiquities room arm in arm. Karl-Heinz Hausen steers her towards one of the display cases. He shows her a royal blue glazed pottery hippopotamus decorated with black floral designs. Stunned she looks at the object. Karl-Heinz Hausen begins speaking at great length. He seems be expounding about the object. Celia Rosenberg looks at the blue hippopotamus. Karl-Heinz Hausen continues to hold forth in German. Celia Rosenberg does not know a single word of German. She says, "You know I don't speak German." He says, "I know." He looks into her eyes.

He points at the little blue hippopotamus in the display case again. He says, "Look." And he begins speaking German again. Celia Rosenberg waits for him to stop. But Karl-Heinz Hausen does not stop. He continues, enunciating clearly, as if she were able to understand what he is saying. She repeats, "I don't speak German." He looks into her eyes, replies, "I know." And begins speaking again. Celia Rosenberg looks at the Egyptian hippopotamus. She wonders what on earth Karl-Heinz Hausen is talking about. She wonders why Karl-Heinz Hausen insists on speaking German to her when she doesn't understand German.

She asks, "Parlez-vous français?" Karl-Heinz Hausen replies, "Non." And he starts speaking again. He talks on endlessly. Celia Rosenberg sets off towards the next room. Karl-Heinz Hausen immediately catches hold of her arm, his green eyes gaze into Celia Rosenberg's grey ones. He says, "Bitte," in a low voice. Celia Rosenberg retraces her steps, stations herself in front of the blue hippopotamus's case. She says, "So, the story?" Karl-Heinz Hausen smiles at her, begins speaking again.

She listens. She thinks that maybe he is a specialist. Most likely a specialist. Perhaps Karl-Heinz Hausen was an egyptologist before the war. She asks, "Were you an egyptologist before the war?" He replies, "Bitte?" She doesn't insist. He resumes his lecture. Celia Rosenberg wonders if he is talking about hippopotamuses in particular or Egypt in general. She watches him as he speaks. He is very handsome. His face lights up as he no doubt evokes landscapes, temples, statuary, an entire civilisation which, who knows, has been his passion since childhood. She watches him as he speaks but he does not stop nor does he seem about to.

Suddenly, in the middle of an unintelligible sentence, a lump forms in Celia Rosenberg's chest. Her vision blurs, her heart beats very fast. Celia Rosenberg is suddenly gripped by a feeling of intense dread as she listens to the German soldier lecture about the little blue hippopotamus in the Egyptian Antiquities room. The room is deserted. Only the surly attendant's footsteps echo through the gallery. Karl-Heinz Hausen has stopped talking. He is looking at Celia Rosenberg who is white as a sheet. Her pupils are dilated, she is short of breath. He clasps her to his breast, murmurs, "You understand," and places a kiss on her ear.

Celia Rosenberg is feeling better. She takes a big breath, says she wants to get some fresh air. The green magician follows her as she goes from room to room, almost at a run, pulling Karl-Heinz Hausen with her. He obeys her, distraught. They walk in the Louvre courtyard. He stops, pulls her to him, kisses her. She immerses herself in the kiss, melts in his arms. She can feel Karl-

Heinz Hausen's erection through their clothes and desire sweeps
through her deliciously. She begins telling him about herself.
About her and him. Her love for him. Her desire for him.
Karl-Heinz Hausen has loosened his embrace; he is listen-
ing to her. Celia Rosenberg talks about her mother left alone in
Alsace. Her brother Julian whom they don't hear from any more.
When she says, "Julian" her voice shakes a little. Karl-Heinz
Hausen looks at her. They have started walking again, slowly.

They walk in the Tuileries and, as they walk, Celia Rosenberg, immersed in her thoughts, talks, looking straight ahead.
Karl-Heinz Hausen does not understand French but she knows
he is listening to her. So she talks. She speaks as she has never
spoken to anyone before. Unless to Julian, when they were very
young. She tells Karl-Heinz Hausen how she and Julian loved
dressing up when they were little. She describes Julian with his
little policeman's cape, their father's kepi and an elder branch
for a saber. She says how funny he looked with the flowering
branch that didn't look at all like a saber but that he insisted on
using for their fierce battles. She describes the flounced, blue
polka dot dress she wore to dance fiery flamencos on the sloping
lawn of the family home. Celia Rosenberg laughs softly, her eyes
sparkling with mischief, as she recalls these games. Karl-Heinz
Hausen walks beside her, receptive to the emotions revealed by
her voice. He takes Celia Rosenberg's hand, squeezes it. She
turns towards him and says, "You understand, don't you?" He
replies, "I understand." Celia Rosenberg sighs with pleasure.

They walk on in silence. They look at the trees. The sky is
grey. There is a strong wind, bitterly cold, as if it were November. Karl-Heinz Hausen begins speaking, very slowly at first,
falling silent from time to time, then taking up his story again.
Probably about his childhood. About Brandenburg. She clearly
makes out the word, "Brandenburg." Karl-Heinz Hausen tells
her about his childhood as they walk along the almost deserted
paths. Celia Rosenberg listens to him passionately, aware of the
slightest change in his voice. She is suddenly overcome by a
wave of sadness. She stops, cradles his head in her hands, presses

her forehead against his and says, "Oh my love..."

Celia Rosenberg absorbs Karl-Heinz Hausen's sadness. A murky wave spins within her heart, waking the pale she-devils lurking in the labyrinth of her own sorrow. She gazes deep into Karl-Heinz Hausen's eyes. Celia Rosenberg has the impression that she has known this man since the dawn of time. There, in the middle of the Tuileries Gardens, she recognizes the anguish in Karl-Heinz Hausen's eyes, that sudden anguish. It is the same anguish. Celia Rosenberg's anguish.

But, Karl-Heinz Hausen's eyes light up with amusement. He bursts out laughing and runs off down the path. Surprised, Celia Rosenberg turns round, watches him run away, laughing. He takes another path to the right and soon disappears behind a hedge. Celia Rosenberg walks solemnly along the main path in the Tuileries Gardens. Sits down on a chair. Looks at the sky. The sky is very grey. Pigeons are pecking at the ground around her. They fly away, grey wings flapping loudly.

Celia Rosenberg takes her gold plated cigarette case out of her grey snakeskin purse. She removes her kid gloves and puts them in her purse. Lights a cigarette with the gold plated lighter Karl-Heinz-Hausen gave her. "Karl- Heinz Hausen," Celia Rosenberg, thinks. "Karl-Heinz Hausen." Filled with joy, she closes her eyes, an incandescent glow casts a white shadow over her. Karl-Heinz Hausen is there before her, dazzled by her pale, grey beauty in the grey day.

She says, "I'm afraid I'll never see you again, Karl-Heinz Hausen." He replies in German. He says that he too is afraid. The chair attendant comes towards them with a vindictive look on her face. Celia Rosenberg gets up quickly, hands her a few francs, begins walking away. Karl-Heinz Hausen is holding her hand in his again. Her fingers are frozen. She is still smoking, blowing the grey cigarette smoke into the cold air. Karl-Heinz Hausen begins speaking again. About Brandenburg. And Berlin. Celia Rosenberg clearly recognizes the word "Berlin." About the first time he went to Berlin as a small boy with his grandfather. About the storybook his grandfather gave him when he had mumps. About Till Eulenspiegel who jingled coins to pay the innkeeper who only allowed him to smell the food. Celia Rosenberg studies the glow of pleasure on Karl-Heinz Hausen's face. She likes the sounds he makes when he speaks, the crisp sound of his saliva, his guttural accent. A feeling of overweening tenderness for this man she does not know sweeps through Celia Rosenberg. She gazes at the love on Karl-Heinz Hausen's face. She sees the joy on his face. She reads passion on it. Celia Rosenberg watches Karl-Heinz Hausen, captivated by his radiant vitality. Like she was by that on Julian's face in the garden on a Thursday in July 1928.

Leaving the path, Sylvia Rosenberg leans her back against a tree and looks up at the sky to stop her tears from falling. Karl-Heinz Hausen has come over to her. He very gently asks her something. She tells him. She tells him about that Thursday in July 1928. The sun that day. How shiny the leaves of the chestnut trees were in her childhood garden in Alsace. She describes her mother's old black shoes that she was wearing as she wandered round the garden with Julian who, joking around, patted her bottom. She tells how angry she was. How furious, with all the indignation of an eight-year-old. She tells how she took off one of the shoes and hit Julian so hard on the forehead with it that he fell over backwards. Celia Rosenberg describes the blood pouring down her little brother's forehead. She says how terrified she was. Tells how dreadfully sorry and ashamed she was. About the interminable hours hiding in the cellar waiting for his murder to be discovered. About how she still suffers dreadfully over an act committed so long ago. She says that Julian didn't die but that thinking for so many hours that he was dead amounted to the same thing. She tells Karl-Heinz Hausen how, after that, she never again refused Julian anything. He became her tyrant, her master, her lover. She describes how passionately she loved her brother Julian and, at the same time, hated him.

Karl-Heinz Hausen's breath caresses her mouth. He listens to her, one hand resting on the bark of the tree, the other in his trouser pocket. A tramp goes past on the path, grumbling. Celia

Rosenberg smiles sadly. She says, "I can see that you appreciate my melodrama as much as I liked yours." Seeing Karl-Heinz Hausen's bewilderment and incomprehension in the face of this sudden irony, Celia Rosenberg's bitterness vanishes. She throws her arms around his neck, kisses him. His sweet breath reminds her of the smell of the pink magnolias which sway in the breeze in the Louisiana of her dreams. Celia Rosenberg and Karl-Heinz Hausen have begun walking again. Celia Rosenberg dances along the path, runs to the big pond and collapses onto a chair.

A little boy, dressed in tweed, is using a long stick to steer a sailboat over the water. He is singing very quietly to himself, completely oblivious to Celia Rosenberg and Karl-Heinz Hausen who has also sat down on a chair. Celia Rosenberg begins talking about Louisiana. She says she has never been to Louisiana. But that Louisiana is paradise. The heat, the magnolias. Particularly the magnolias. Karl-Heinz Hausen repeats: "Magnolia." She bursts out laughing, says, "That's it! Magnolia." And, in her imagination, she rushes down to the blue valley at the bottom of which flows a river so clear that you can see tiny green shrimp swimming in it.

Karl-Heinz Hausen is silent. He watches the clouds gliding across the sky. Clouds of sparrows are perched on the chairs around them. On the other side of the pond an old man is throwing breadcrumbs to the pigeons flying around him. The little boy is running round the pond to catch his sailboat that the wind is pushing along rapidly.

Celia Rosenberg heaves a deep sigh, opens her grey eyes on the grey tableau of the Tuileries. The magnolias disappear. Karl-Heinz Hausen has begun speaking again. He talks about studying at Heidelberg University. About his love of music. About learning to play the violin when he was very young. He also talks about his mother. He tells her about his father's death during the other war, when he was just a baby. He describes the only photo he has ever seen of his father; the others were destroyed in a fire.

She says it is really quite cold for the month of August. There is so little light in the sky today that you would think it was already autumn. "But you are here," she says, turning towards him, "Karl-Heinz Hausen. I like your name, Karl-Heinz Hausen."

He takes Celia Rosenberg's hand in his, looks down at his shoes and says, "Ich liebe Sie, Celia Rosenberg." Celia Rosenberg does not understand German. But she understands these words. They are the exact words of Hans Meyer, "Ich liebe Sie, Celia Rosenberg." They were both ten years old. Then Hans' family had moved to Hamburg. And Celia Rosenberg had stopped understanding German.

She stands up abruptly. She says, "But we'll never see each other again, Karl-Heinz Hausen." She is seized with the desire to start running towards the Concorde and disappear into a taxi. But something holds her back. It is stronger than her, much stronger. She repeats, "We'll never see each other again, Karl-Heinz Hausen." But she doesn't believe it. He raises his eyes to her, says again, "Ich liebe Sie, Celia Rosenberg."

The words free up huge blocks of ice in her heart. They roll around, bump into each other, icebergs released from great depths. Celia Rosenberg feels a sharp pain in her chest. Her vision blurs. Something breaks inside her. She stands erect in her grey costume and grey hat, frozen with pain. Karl-Heinz Hausen says nothing. He doesn't know what to say. Then he says, "Ich liebe Sie, Celia Rosenberg."

She has begun walking very fast. He catches up with her. She is crying bitterly. He kisses her tears, her cheeks, her lips. She calms down. Rests her face on Karl-Heinz Hausen's shoulder. He hands her his handkerchief. She wipes off the mascara which has run. Looks at herself in a little round mirror. A swan is engraved on its rhinestone cover. Karl-Heinz Hausen smiles and says, "Schwan?" She looks at the little mirror, turns it over. Says, "'Schwan': yes, a swan. Yes, 'Schwan.'"

Celia Rosenberg says that the mirror was a gift from her aunt Laure who lives in Paris. She talks about her aunt Laure who is a bit of a magician. She tells him about how excited she was in the Strasbourg-Paris train as it carried her through the night. Celia Rosenberg talks about how, in the dark of the night of November 9, 1938, the golden light from the houses shone like so many stars in the cloudless sky of her dream of glory. Celia Rosenberg wanted to be an actress. She describes how she arrived at her aunt Laure's with her meagre baggage on a warm, sunny November morning. Her happiness as she climbed the steps of Montmartre four at a time, crazy with joy, and how, at the top of the steps, she turned round, opened her arms wide and surveyed the entire district in exaltation, feeling as if all Paris belonged to her.

Karl-Heinz Hausen and Celia Rosenberg navigate the traffic in the Place de la Concorde. Karl-Heinz Hausen leads Celia Rosenberg towards the Luxor obelisk. He begins studying the column close up. She asks, "Were you an egyptologist before the war?" He does not answer. It starts drizzling. By the time they have run for shelter, the rain has already stopped.

They are now strolling along the Cours-la-Reine. Karl-Heinz Hausen is interested in the *bateaux mouches* gliding along the grey waters of the Seine. Celia Rosenberg is talking about her aunt Laure who is teaching her to see things in a crystal ball and read tarot cards. She says that was when she began seeing the green magician in mirrors and in the water. Karl-Heinz Hausen has made his way towards the Pont Alexandre III. She follows him. Towards the middle of the bridge they stop, watch the water flow beneath them. Celia Rosenberg gives a start when she sees the green magician, holding on to one of the pillars of the bridge, baring her teeth.

Celia Rosenberg cannot help seeing this as a bad omen. She shivers. Is overcome by a grim foreboding, averts her eyes. Karl-Heinz Hausen is leaning on the parapet his face resting on his fists, contemplating the Seine. Celia Rosenberg chases away her gloomy thoughts. After all, the Germans have been in Paris since June. What worse can happen?

For the first time, Celia Rosenberg no longer sees Karl-

Heinz Hausen as a customer, a lover, an object of love, but as an enemy soldier. The sudden shock of this realisation leaves her rooted to the spot. The grey water continues to flow under the Pont Alexandre III. Heavy grey clouds are approaching. Celia Rosenberg remembers yesterday afternoon's storm. She also remembers her ecstasy in Karl-Heinz Hausen's arms. "*Luxe, calme et volupté...*" Celia Rosenberg thinks. She asks, "Have you read Baudelaire?" Karl-Heinz Hausen raises his eyebrows questioningly.

She links her arm through his and recites *L'Invitation au voyage*. He listens, spellbound. Soon they are walking along the Left Bank of the Seine. Furious passers by give them scathing looks. But Celia Rosenberg finishes the poem with a magnificent lyrical flourish. Karl-Heinz Hausen has stopped to applaud her. An elderly woman calls out as she passes them, "Shame on you, reciting Baudelaire to a Kraut!" Defiantly, Celia Rosenberg moves close to Karl-Heinz Hausen, puts her arms around him melodramatically, kisses him passionately. He laughs, frees himself. The woman has stopped indignantly and is staring at them. He takes Celia Rosenberg onto the rue Fabert, shaking off the offended Parisian woman who, grumbling, seemed about to follow them.

They wander around the little streets for a long time, retracing their steps, going round in circles. As evening falls they finally emerge in front of the Eiffel Tower. Karl-Heinz Hausen gives an admiring whistle. Celia Rosenberg says that she too was overcome with wonder the first time she saw it. She says that she came with her cousin Pascal, a fourteen-year-old little horror, devilishly handsome and cunning as a fox. She tells him that he gave her the fright of her life, getting her to climb the Eiffel Tower. She says that, since she didn't want to tarnish her cousin's unfailing devotion to her, she grabbed onto the metal structure with false bravery, paying no attention to the other visitors' stunned expressions as they ogled her underwear, seemingly delighting in the spectacle. She describes how she went higher and higher, following the boy as he climbed with remarkable agility.

Tells how she lost her footing and, clinging to a girder, hung for a few seconds between earth and sky before regaining a foothold. Pascal, who had seen it all, waved and called out to her. Celia Rosenberg recounts how she began her ascent again in spite of orders from the police who were running in all directions on the stairs.

She bursts out laughing. Karl-Heinz Hausen and Celia Rosenberg disappear into the elevator and rise above the City of Light which is beginning to glow in the evening mist. When they emerge from the escalator on the top floor of the Eiffel Tower, all Paris is glistening, grey. The winding Seine, a long, shiny, very black, liquid snake, glitters like black diamonds beneath the glow of the street lamps. Karl-Heinz Hausen and Celia Rosenberg hug, crazy with desire for each other, madly in love. You wouldn't say there was a war.

You wouldn't say there was a war. But you can feel it. Celia Rosenberg tightens her grip on Karl-Heinz Hausen's arm. She feels as if she is swaying in space, between the sky and the earth: she is suddenly overcome with dizziness and nausea. She can see the crowd again below her, the trees, the Seine glistening in the sunshine. And, above her, Pascal laughing and waving at her. Fear takes hold of Celia Rosenberg; the fear that she didn't feel two years earlier hits her now, while she is safe on the platform. A vague, latent, deeply buried fear.

Celia Rosenberg turns her back on the lights of Paris, faces Karl-Heinz Hausen. She looks into his eyes. Celia Rosenberg describes how, through Lola-Valérie, Pascal's girlfriend, she met Gracia von Hendricks, an exiled Berliner and left-wing intellectual, who swears only by Berthold Brecht, a young, practically unknown German author whose play she was preparing to put on in a small theatre in the fifth district. Celia Rosenberg explains that through their meeting, she got a small part in *The Threepenny Opera*. She describes the excitement of the rehearsals, Gracia von Hendricks' monumental outbreaks of anger at the lack of talent of the young actors and actresses, all amateurs, all equally ambitious and inept.

Karl-Heinz Hausen listens quietly to Celia Rosenberg. The timbre of her voice changes as she talks about those few exciting months before the declaration of war. Gracia von Hendricks had quickly recognized her talent and was preparing to give her a bigger role, replacing one of the young actresses whom she considered increasingly incompetent as the rehearsals progressed. But the declaration of war put paid to the project and Gracia von Hendricks had to give up her dream.

Celia Rosenberg relates how, on the day when the troop had just learned the news with dismay and Gracia von Hendricks, in tears, had retreated into silence, Maurice Pons appeared. Tall, dark-haired with a brooding air, the young man, elegantly dressed in a summer suit, immediately impressed Celia Rosenberg. Was it his white silk scarf, his kid gloves, the enigmatic warmth of his smile when he saw her? Celia Rosenberg fell under his thrall immediately.

He was young Lola-Valérie's new boyfriend. She had just ditched Pascal for this more prestigious representative of the male sex. Celia Rosenberg had trouble hiding her emotions. Although distraught, Gracia von Hendricks warned her, "Be careful. Maurice Pons is a wolf."

"Yes. Maurice Pons is a wolf," Celia Rosenberg looks Karl-Heinz Hausen straight in the eye and says, "He is the owner of the nightclub where you met me." Karl-Heinz Hausen doesn't understand what Celia Rosenberg is saying but he listens to her. He knows she is talking to him. It doesn't matter what she is saying. She is talking to him. As she continues her voice becomes increasingly charged with emotion and tension, but also seems more and more present. As if what she is recalling is becoming more substantial, brushing against her like shadows in the strong wind that is tugging at her clothes as she tells her story, holding her hat with both hands, her gaze fixed on the German soldier's green eyes, her back turned on the lights of Paris.

Celia Rosenberg describes how, after adroitly making Lola-Valérie disappear from the scene for a while, Maurice Pons set about seducing her. She recounts how, already conquered, she did not take long to fall passionately in love with him, when, playing the gentleman, he began regularly sending her dozens of tea roses and taking her to fashionable nightclubs to drink champagne. How, before long, Maurice Pons opened his own nightclub – Chez Filou – where Lola-Valérie and she were hired as "hostesses." Celia Rosenberg tells how, captivated by the handsome pimp, they quickly developed a taste for the nightlife, the easy life they led as high-class prostitutes, partners in their vulnerability to the pernicious charm of an increasingly brutal Maurice Pons.

"It's lucky Lola-Valérie is there," Celia Rosenberg says affectionately. "Without her, I would have thrown myself into the Seine in the first days of that life of hell and heaven, excess and despair, filthy lucre and false frivolity." Karl-Heinz Hausen bursts out laughing inappropriately. "What are you laughing at?" Celia Rosenberg asks as he takes her by the shoulders and pulls her towards the elevator.

Celia Rosenberg falls silent as the Eiffel Tower elevator takes them back to ground level. She is thinking about Lola-Valérie. She is thinking about Maurice Pons. Celia Rosenberg grits her teeth, nursing her resentment. She relives the moment when he slapped her hard because she refused to take home Vassilio who was dead drunk but rolling in money. Celia Rosenberg broods over her humiliation and anger. Karl-Heinz Hausen is gazing into space distractedly.

Celia Rosenberg approaches him and says, her voice hoarse, "we will never see each other again, Karl-Heinz Hausen." But, as they cross the Pont d'Iéna her body is suddenly swept by such heat that she sways on her high heels in the violent, freezing wind. He has come to a halt in front of her. Radiating love and sadness he takes her by the shoulders and clasps her to him. She says "I love you, Karl-Heinz Hausen." He lets go of her, sneers. Now Karl-Heinz Hausen is looking at Celia Rosenberg so contemptuously that she feels his stare will kill her, right there, right then, on the Pont d'Iéna. He is seeing the hooker now. The loose woman, the lustful devil who gives herself to anyone, sells her body for money, stirs up desire and sucks the life blood out of the soul. Celia Rosenberg can clearly see the green magician's grin in Karl-Heinz Hausen's crazed gaze. He is in the grip of a hatred that cuts right through her.

Celia Rosenberg breaks down beneath the weight of this hatred. She cries out in terror. Karl-Heinz Hausen covers Celia Rosenberg's mouth with his hand. She bites Karl-Heinz Hausen's hand, frees herself and runs to the illuminated fountains at Trocadero. He catches up with her there, mad with rage. He yells in German. He hurls obscenities at her, slaps her.

Celia Rosenberg reacts immediately. She slaps him back. He is taken aback. Celia Rosenberg starts speaking very calmly. She says it is obvious he has an image of her that he wants to annihilate. Says she is not that image. She says, "We will never see each other again, Karl-Heinz Hausen." He weeps.

Celia Rosenberg turns on her heel. Walks towards the Pont d'Iéna, crosses it again. She is trembling all over, still shaken by cold anger. Celia Rosenberg knows that she hates this man. She is shivering with cold and would like to die. Hate travels through her, like liquid acid.

Suddenly, as if in spite of herself, Celia Rosenberg turns round, runs back across the Pont d'Iéna. Karl-Heinz Hausen is waiting for her with his hands in his pockets, looking furious. But Celia Rosenberg knows that his anger is simply the opposite face of his sadness. Love floods through her again, carries her pain away. She approaches Karl-Heinz Hausen slowly, holds out her hand to him. He takes her cold hand, kisses it. Tears are running down his cheeks. Celia Rosenberg leads him away. They walk for a long time hand in hand in silence along the banks of the Seine.

Celia Rosenberg is thinking about Clara La Brune who, one slow evening at Chez Filou, talked to her at length about passion. The old prostitute, her gypsy eyes shining with mystery and wisdom, repeated tirelessly, in her strong Romanian accent, that passion has its price. Still a radiant beauty, comfortable with her fifty years, the enigmatic Clara La Brune never divulges anything about the passions she has doubtless known. But she loves talking about passion as if it were a brilliant abstraction that her gaze follows in the cloud of bluish smoke suspended in the air of the nightclub. Celia Rosenberg forgets the reassuring musky scent of her old friend, as her mind returns to walking beneath the dim yellow light of the street lamps on that inordinately cold evening on August 16, 1940 with the German soldier with whom she has fallen suddenly, irrationally, passionately in love.

Karl-Heinz Hausen can see Grete's disarming smile as she shakes her heavy auburn locks, denying that she has accepted Professor Erhard's invitation to lunch with such candour that his distrust and jealousy were immediately swept away. He lets out a sigh of grief at the thought of Grete's betrayal. It will take him months to get over it.

Holding hands, Celia Rosenberg and Karl-Heinz Hausen stroll idly along the Seine, miserable, tormented, vaguely happy. They are overwhelmed by such waves of contradictory feelings that they both remain obstinately silent, focused on the emotional turmoil raging within them.

Suddenly, Celia Rosenberg feels, like a physical pain, that in barely an hour, they will be separated. In an hour she could be crying over this man whom she loves and beside whom she is walking, locked in angry, stubborn silence.

As they reach the Pont de Grenelle, Celia Rosenberg pulls Karl-Heinz Hausen into the allée des Cygnes. It is deserted. She begins speaking, her voice barely audible. She talks about love. She puts her cold hands on Karl-Heinz Hausen's face, strokes his neck. She murmurs excuses, begs his forgiveness, launches into such an orgy of guilt and despair that Karl-Heinz Hausen, unable to bear it any more, steps back, starts shouting at the top of his voice. He shouts that he loves her, that he is madly in love, that he resents her for it, that he detests her, that he doesn't want to love her. He shouts that they are at war. He screams that she is a dirty Jew.

Celia Rosenberg endures this outburst of anger without a word. She goes up to Karl-Heinz Hausen, her finger to her lips to silence him. She says she belongs to only him, forever, for eternity. To only him. To nobody else but him. She brings her lips close to his, slides her tongue into Karl-Heinz Hausen's mouth, kisses him feverishly. He returns the kiss, pulls her against his chest and circles her with his arms. Their defences melt away with the warmth of their bodies, they find love again, the breathless fire of love, the beating heart of passion. They exchange words of love, lick each other's faces, become heavy with desire and tenderness at the idea that in barely an hour they will be separated.

The allée des Cygnes stretches, a dark shadow in the middle of the Seine, its surface sparkling as if scattered by a myriad tiny stars. Karl-Heinz Hausen is looking at Celia Rosenberg's profile. She reminds him of that Egyptian queen whose portrait is engraved on a fragment of the Karnak obelisk that he has studied at length. Solemn, pale and grey Celia Rosenberg is walking beside him like Hatshepsut herself. Karl-Heinz Hausen knows that he wants this woman.

Gabrielle Lévy

Brandenburg, November 11, 1943. It is almost nightfall. Seated at the window, Celia Rosenberg watches night creep over the little fieldstone wall enclosed garden surrounding Frau Hausen's house which is pleasantly situated on a hill on the edge of the town. Frau Hausen is not yet back from her job in the Management Department of Mittledeutsch Stahlwerk, a big steel works a few kilometers from Brandenburg.

Celia Rosenberg is alone in the big empty house which smells of laundry. Schnee, a pretty, rather nervous white cat, is meowing desperately to be let into the house. Celia Rosenberg goes slowly towards the door, lets in the cat who meows with renewed vigour and rubs against her ankles. The animal raises big green eyes towards her imploringly. Unsure of what she wants, Celia Rosenberg picks the cat up. She meows even louder, escapes and runs away. Celia Rosenberg sits back down in the fading light. The sharp pain in her chest is still there, cutting like a knife.

The good smell from before the war wafts from the cabbage soup that she made earlier in the afternoon. Simmering on a low heat, it fills the house with warmth and peaceful happiness. Celia Rosenberg remembers the smell of cabbage that greeted her like an outpouring of family love when she came home from the local school, exhausted by her long walk. She breathes in deeply, lifting her ribs as if to free herself from the weight that has been oppressing her for so long that, on some days, she is able to forget its constant presence.

She finds a little comfort in recalling more peaceful times. But immediately, she gives a start at the memory of her mother, standing on the balcony, anxiously wringing her hands. She wants to drive out that image at all costs. However, it refuses to disappear: she sees everything again in detail. The brown wool dress, too elegant for the occasion, her mother's prematurely grey hair, her distraught air as Celia Rosenberg disappears into the "*traction avant*" where Karl-Heinz Hausen is waiting for her. She feels a pang of anguish that makes the pain in her chest worse.

Celia Rosenberg sees herself on the same balcony a few months earlier, scolding her brother, Julian, in no uncertain terms for enlisting in the German army under the name of Hans Rodan. Celia Rosenberg is accusing him of being hardhearted because he refuses to help them cross into Switzerland. But Julian retorts that she can insult him as much as she likes, nothing will stop him from joining his lover in Strasbourg. Schnee has jumped onto Celia Rosenberg's knees and she strokes her automatically, her gaze fixed on the dark window, lost in a wave of sadness.

Soon, the cat falls asleep, purring. Celia Rosenberg nurses her sorrow, eyes closed, her lips set in a bitter line. She thinks about Karl-Heinz Hausen. She pictures him arriving unexpectedly, throwing his cap across the room, picking her up happily. But no one has come in. Only shadows creeping silently. Celia Rosenberg sighs, begins singing softly for the child in her belly. Schnee sniffs and jumps down to chase an imaginary mouse.

Celia Rosenberg falls into a sort of shadowy half sleep. She pictures herself putting Karl-Heinz Hausen's boots on her bare feet in her Paris bedroom. She sees herself daydreaming in the synagogue, eager to meet Hans Meyer again. She pictures her two-year-old self on the cold kitchen tiles, busy trying to catch a ray of sunshine. The pictures line up side-by-side, become entangled, follow each other incongruously, superimpose themselves to form a sort of long twisted snake with a paper spine. The daguerreotypes pile one on top of the other, give way and collapse into a mental labyrinth which makes her dizzy. Celia Rosenberg opens her eyes on the blank window. She calls the cat, "Schnee, Schnee!" The cat comes bounding over, gives a heartrending wail, jumps onto Celia Rosenberg's lap and begins purring deliriously.

As she strokes the white fur, Celia Rosenberg drifts among perfumed pink magnolias swaying in the breeze. But imperious meowing drives her out of her enchanted Louisiana. Celia Rosenberg's grey eyes gaze into the cat's dark ones, a flame piercing the darkness. She says, "What's wrong, little cat?" The regal Schnee replies with a mournful cry of despair.

Celia Rosenberg is suddenly back in front of the lit up Christmas tree, opening the wicker basket that Karl-Heinz Hausen has given her. To her great surprise, a tiny, irresistible, pure white kitten raised its head, opened its little pink mouth from which came the most delightful meows she has ever heard. A sort of staccato cry, languorous and cruel, between a baby's wail and the raucous quacking of an ugly little duckling. She became attached to the creature immediately and named her *Blanche Neige*. Frau Hausen persisted in calling her Schnee and since it was completely impossible for the older woman to pronounce the French sounds, Celia Rosenberg came round to adopting that name. It conjured up the image of a white-haired being that suited the lyrical little cat. From the outset, Celia Rosenberg sometimes caught a glimpse of the terrifying magician in the liquid green eyes full of mystery through which Schnee regarded everything from her first days on earth.

For some obscure reason, Schnee calms down, curls up on Celia Rosenberg's lap, begins purring loudly again and sinks into her dreams. The warmth of the animal against her belly reminds the young woman that life has been forming in that belly for almost three months. Taking a deep breath, Celia Rosenberg makes her still relatively flat abdomen swell unnaturally. She feels as round as the earth, liquid, warm, the bearer of an extraordinary miracle beyond her comprehension. Happiness courses through her veins; Celia Rosenberg begins singing the loving song again that she has invented specially for Frank or Gisela growing in her warm womb, sheltered from cold, hunger and the war. Shielded from sadness. Celia Rosenberg flees sadness like the plague. She wants the bright peace of the heights for her child. She envelops the cat with love making her stretch voluptuously.

Later, Celia Rosenberg gets up carefully, holding the cat in her arms. Schnee wriggles furiously to free herself, meowing heartrendingly. Celia Rosenberg lets the cat leap onto the chair where she curls up. She lights a fire in the big fireplace in the lounge. Sitting back on her heels, Celia Rosenberg gazes into the dancing flames. The heat from the fire comforts her. Winged horses gallop in Schnee's big green eyes as she sits in front of the fire gazing into the flames.

Eyes closed, Celia Rosenberg's lets the Louisiana sun burnish her face. She soaks in the light and breathes in the sweet air, perfumed by magnolia pollen. Tall green grass stretches into the distance beneath a powder blue sky. She crosses the grassland. On the other side, the green magician is standing in a stream, eyeing her scornfully. Frightened, Celia Rosenberg opens her eyes. She moves closer to the fire, sits down comfortably on the sheepskin in front of the fireplace. The white cat immediately joins her.

Celia Rosenberg is thinking about Karl-Heinz Hausen. His absence is so painful, so cruel, that most of the time she doesn't think about it. But, all day today his absence has weighed heavily on her. She gets up, walks into her bedroom. In the firelight, the bed, covered by a thick white duvet is barely discernible in the shadows. Celia Rosenberg stretches out on it. She remembers the intense white light flooding the bedroom in the middle of a moonless night in August when Karl-Heinz Hausen made love to her for the last time. The following day he was leaving for a new posting. Celia Rosenberg's body stiffens painfully at the thought that Karl-Heinz Hausen does not even know she is expecting his child.

The cat is prowling around the bed giving small, high-pitched cries that set Celia Rosenberg's nerves on edge. Forcing herself to stay calm, she bends down to the cat, asks her what is wrong. Schnee continues her performance with exasperating shrill meows. Celia Rosenberg tells her to stop caterwauling and to follow her into the kitchen. She mashes potatoes and milk and puts the mixture in the cat's bowl. She goes back to sit in front of the fire. The cat turns up her nose at the food and circles her, yowling.

Celia Rosenberg puts Schnee on her knees and, holding her front paws, looks straight into her eyes. The green magician, taken aback, stares at her from the depths of the white cat's eyes. Celia Rosenberg says, "So, what do you want from me?" She trembles with horror when she sees the green magician's lips curl back in a snarl revealing black gums. She puts the struggling cat down and, holding her breath, gazes into the fire.

The door opens. Looking tired but radiant for some mysterious reason, Frau Hausen smiles at her. Celia Rosenberg soon understands why she is so happy: Karl-Heinz Hausen's mother takes a loaf out of her shopping bag. "No doubt she got it on the black market," Celia Rosenberg thinks as she helps unpack the meagre provisions.

After eating cabbage soup, boiled potatoes, bread and cheese the two women hurry to turn on the radio. Reception is particularly bad this evening but Celia Rosenberg clings to these intonations in a foreign language and the static, which, although she understands absolutely nothing, seem to connect her to Karl-Heinz Hausen who is doubtless also listening to the news. Frau Hausen listens eagerly and anxiously to news which, from one day to the next, leave her more and more perplexed. Celia Rosenberg, watching her face, follows the news but understands nothing. However, an uneasy feeling creeps over her, weighing her down with a dark knowledge she cannot recognize. Day after day, Celia Rosenberg waits for the end of the war to be announced. Day after day nothing happens. Day after day she hopes. "This war is sure to end one day," Celia Rosenberg thinks. At the same time, visions of eternal hell make her shiver in the kitchen that is dimly lit by a bulb that flickers then goes out for good.

Frau Hausen curses the electricity cut, climbs onto a chair, grabs an oil lamp from the top of the cupboard and busies herself lighting it. The chimney is immediately covered in soot. Frau Hausen adjusts the lamp irritably. Celia Rosenberg takes her hand and smiles at her. Frau Hausen nods, smiles back. She washes the dishes while Celia Rosenberg wipes the table. No sooner is this done than Schnee leaps onto it, threatening to knock the lamp over. "Shnell Schnee!" Celia Rosenberg shouts angrily. Frau Hausen bursts out laughing.

For an instant Celia Rosenberg thinks she sees the steely gaze of the green woman flare up in the German woman's pale eyes. She wipes her sweat-covered brow wearily. The hallucination is taking over more and more of her being. "No doubt I have a bit of a temperature," Celia Rosenberg thinks, picking up her knitting. She is knitting wool socks for Karl-Heinz Hausen. Frau Hausen looks up from her work, anxiously. But Celia Rosenberg hastens to reassure her with her most radiant smile. Relieved, Karl-Heinz Hausen's mother goes back to counting stitches, her lips moving slightly.

Around 10 o'clock, the two women make verbena tea and drink it in silence before retiring to their respective bedrooms for the night.

Schnee is already asleep, rolled in a ball on Celia Rosenberg's bed. Outside the fog has lifted and the full moon is shining through the lace-curtained window. Celia Rosenberg undresses slowly, slips into a flannel nightgown, "not at all Parisian," she thinks nostalgically. She remembers the tangerine silk negligee Léopold Schwann had given her in the hope that she would finally forget the German officer with whom she had become so infatuated that, during his lengthy absences, she sank into depression. Celia Rosenberg, eyes wide open in the German night, wonders what has become of Léopold Schwann. The last time she saw him was... in 1941. Yes, in 1941. At Sarah de Mouliac's in October 1941. Celia Rosenberg remembers the rain lashing down behind the heavy black velvet drapes. The guests' false gaiety, the champagne, the sparkling crystal and jewellery. She vaguely remembers Laurence crying because of the executions that have just been carried out in Bordeaux. Laurence saying that they absolutely have to do something, that they cannot let this happen. Celia Rosenberg is trying to calm down a trembling, moaning Laurence. Clara La Brune's voice reaches them from the reception room. Her hoarse, sad voice rises then suddenly breaks off. Celia Rosenberg catches the look in Jeff's eye, the expression of a wounded animal. The elegant young man, his distress unmasked, slips behind a group of overexcited young women surrounding Jeanne Morin.

Celia Rosenberg gives a start. How could she have forgotten Jeanne Morin. The memory jolts her out of the half-sleep that was overtaking her. She remembers Jeanne with a bandage on her head, that evening, at Sarah de Mouliac's. Celia Rosenberg seems to remember that there had been a spiritualist séance that evening. A distraught Julian holding Jeanne Morin's arm to clear the way for her through the guests who were trying to corner her for a personal consultation. Jeanne Morin recognized Celia Rosenberg, whom she has met several times at her aunt Laure's and nodded slightly at her. In her dark Gypsy eyes, Celia Rosenberg saw the green magician flee.

Léopold Schwann, brimming with confidence, waltzes her smoothly beneath the chandeliers in the reception room. She breathes in his pleasing scent of leather and high-quality cigars. Celia Rosenberg abandons herself to the pleasure of dancing. For a few short minutes, she forgets. But the pain she can see in Emmanuelle's eyes reminds her. Karl-Heinz Hausen, Karl-Heinz Hausen, where are you, Karl-Heinz Hausen? Feverish, Celia Rosenberg finds herself sitting up in her bed. The dark sky outlined against the window is dimly lit by the milky whiteness of the full moon.

Emmanuelle also loved a young German soldier. Fritz. Celia Rosenberg remembers Fritz. In July. Yes, in the middle of July, in Paris. It was very hot. On her left, Léopold Schwann was drinking his soup noisily. She wasn't hungry. It was so hot. It was in 1942. Yes, in '42. Was that really the last time she had seen Léopold? Fritz was seated on her right. Celia Rosenberg cannot remember what the young German soldier was doing there. In her memory, Emmanuelle is not seated at that table. Emmanuelle is spinning round in Jeff's arms beneath the chandeliers in Sarah de Mouliak's mansion. Emmanuelle's image is spinning in her soup while Fritz talks to her about Karl-Heinz Hausen and Werner Gabel who has just joined the Afrika Corps. Celia Rosenberg is trying to find out more about Karl-Heinz Hausen but the young soldier pretends not to understand her and revels in detailing their regimental escapades which Celia Rosenberg does not appreciate in the least. Her cousin, Gunther, watches ironically as she gets bogged down in the flood of bad French. Celia Rosenberg asks him furiously if he, in his immense wisdom, has any idea of what is going on. Gunther shrugs his shoulders pretentiously, downs his glass of white wine and, satisfied, winks teasingly at his cousin. The conversation shifts to the owner of the bistro who is making her way between the tables, her arms loaded with full plates.

A wave of nausea hits Celia Rosenberg. She implores her cousin Gunther, "What's going on? What are we doing here, Gunther? Is there a conspiracy?" Celia Rosenberg meets her mother Rebecca's, alarmed look. She seems to have heard the question. Gunther speaks loudly and clearly to Celia Rosenberg assuring her that no one is listening to them. He says it is quite simple: Monsieur Nicolas, the butcher's assistant, has come to dinner wearing his apron. Only then does Celia Rosenberg notice the bloodstained apron. The fat, chubby-cheeked man has even kept his beret on. He has finished drinking his soup and is waiting sulkily for someone to bring his sausages. Then Gunther says, "It's me, Gunther, don't you recognize me?" Celia Rosenberg cannot help smiling. Suddenly, the scene in the bistro fades. Celia Rosenberg feels as if she is falling head first through time. But her cousin's sarcastic laugh brings her back to reality. She suddenly feels terribly fond of her wicked cousin who is telling her to look at her mother. Rebecca is giving her a dark, reproachful look. Celia Rosenberg would like to explain herself. She would like to explain everything. But she doesn't know how. She doesn't know. A terrifying sense of anguish sweeps over Celia Rosenberg. The young blonde woman seated at the end of the table smiles, tells her gently that no doubt her mother would like to see her eat with more relish. Stunned, Celia Rosenberg brings a spoonful of soup to her lips. Rebecca Rosenberg smiles, visibly relieved. Gunther bursts out laughing at the surprised look on Celia Rosenberg's face. The sweet young woman wearing a blue jacket says her name is Mariette Dupont and that she is from Normandy. Celia Rosenberg feels as if she has known her for a long time. Her eyes sparkle mischievously and her fine blonde hair shines in the last rays of sunshine as they cast a feeble light on the terrace. It is so hot! Then Celia Rosenberg turns towards Léopold Schwann. He puts his hand on Celia Rosenberg's thigh. She is wearing a straight black skirt and a sheer, pink silk blouse. The man gives her a look filled with desire that reassures her. But it seems clear that he too does not understand what is happening. Only Gunther, laughing, wide awake and cynical seems to be aware of what is going on. No. Mariette Dupont is still smiling as she eats her sole bonne femme with relish. Rebecca is looking at her daughter's untouched plate in despair. Fritz, his cheeks on fire, is laughing heartily at a joke Gunther has just played on him. Monsieur Nicolas is staring at his already empty plate. Léopold lights a cigar. Nothing is happening. Nothing.

Why is she remembering that scene in so much detail? Now Celia Rosenberg is out of bed pacing the damp tiles in her room. Suddenly she can hear Gunther's voice again. He is looking her straight in the eyes, forcing her to pay attention to him. He says that they are talking about Gabrielle Lévy now, that they all know her. Celia Rosenberg feels a weight on her back. As if invisible hands were pushing her hard. She holds tight to the bistro table with both hands, but they seem to pass through the solid table. Celia Rosenberg disappears into her cousin Gunther's face and the blue flowered wallpaper on the wall against which he is leaning.

The green magician is running beneath the pink magnolias and Celia Rosenberg, out of breath, is running after her. She feels light as a butterfly as she bounds high over the deep green, springy grass. Suddenly she finds herself face-to-face with the magician who stops her in midflight and, gesturing with her raised hands, makes her back away at great speed as if she were being pulled by a magnet. Frightened, she closes her eyes.

The rain is lashing against the windows behind the heavy black velvet drapes. It is October 28, 1941, Sarah de Mouliak's birthday. Celia Rosenberg listens to the rain falling and thinks about Karl-Heinz Hausen. She is watching the champagne bubbles in her glass. Suddenly, a woman speaks to her. An imposing, beautiful blonde of about fifty. A woman with eyes like a cat's. A woman who is speaking to her about the green magician whom she says she can see in Celia Rosenberg's eyes. Celia Rosenberg draws back, frightened. "My dear, don't be afraid. You didn't know that you had the gift?" Celia Rosenberg would like to run far, very far away from this woman who can read her eyes.

"You won't be able to escape from the power, darling, you may as well give up right now." Celia Rosenberg wonders what the old fool is driving at. In spite of herself, she hides a smile behind her glass of champagne. Anastasie Nabokov and Lola-Valérie are coming up the stairs. Standing on the landing, Celia Rosenberg gives them a charming smile, hoping to create a diversion. The woman touches her forearm to make her look at her and says, "My name is Gabrielle Lévy. We'll certainly have the opportunity to see each other again." Turning her back on Celia Rosenberg she begins walking down the stairs. A few steps further down, however, she turns round and, making sure that Anastasia and Lola-Valérie hear her, declares, "Yes he was an egyptologist before the war."

Dumbfounded, Celia Rosenberg drops her glass of champagne which shatters on the floor. Resting her burning forehead

against her bedroom window in Brandenburg, Celia Rosenberg
hears the deafening crash of the crystal glass breaking on a mar-
ble floor in Paris two years earlier. The green magician is dancing in the mist. Celia Rosenberg's feet are cold and her chest
hurts, hurts so badly. An egyptologist. Before the war. Celia Rosenberg emerges
suddenly from her lethargy. She is suddenly hot. She tears off
her white flannel nightgown and stretches, completely naked,
in front of the window open to the night.

She is walking in the fog. In November, in Berlin. Tightly
wrapped in her blue wool coat, Celia Rosenberg is looking for
the address Karl-Heinz Hausen left with his mother. Night has
already fallen when she finally arrives in front of the gate at 12
Amselstrasse. Taking her courage in both hands, Celia Rosenberg rings the doorbell. A few minutes later, a smiling Karl-
Heinz Hausen, in full dress uniform, opens the door. The smile
disappears as soon as he recognizes Celia Rosenberg. He is furious. As he brings her indoors, he says, "You know only too
well that it's dangerous for Jews!" She says no, she doesn't know.
He slaps her. She slaps him back.

They stand looking at each other in silence. Then Karl-
Heinz Hausen leads Celia Rosenberg into a charming small
lounge. He asks her, almost politely to wait for him. She waits.
An open book on a lacquered wood coffee table attracts her attention. She looks at it, curious to know what he is reading. It is
in German, obviously; she doesn't understand any of it. On the
next page, an old engraving by someone called Vivant Denon,
shows the Sphinx surrounded by workers digging the sand out
from around it. Celia Rosenberg quickly closes her eyes because
the book seems to be catching fire and the frightful heat rising
from the flaming lion roaring a few meters away in the desert
makes her double over with pain.

Celia Rosenberg opens her eyes to the coolness of the Brandenburg night, remembers that the author's name on the spine
of the book, stunned her. It was Karl-Heinz Hausen. He had indeed been an egyptologist before the war. Gabrielle Lévy was

right. Gabrielle Lévy had seen it. And what if Gabrielle Lévy was right about the rest too?

Celia Rosenberg is crying, curled up in a ball under the feather duvet. She is still whimpering when she sees Karl-Heinz Hausen reappear in full dress uniform. He is just as furious as when she arrived unexpectedly. Celia Rosenberg takes his hand, asks: "Were you an egyptologist before the war?" The expression in Karl-Heinz Hausen's green eyes softens. He pulls Celia Rosenberg to him, brushes his lips against her neck in a gentle kiss. Then he takes her upstairs, explains that she has to hide because the guests will be arriving soon.

Later, when the guests were already pretty tipsy, they made love among the fur coats. Karl-Heinz Hausen, who was also drunk, was crazy enough to bring a bottle and two glasses of champagne that they drank before he threw her on the bed to take her roughly, fully clothed, both devastating and delighting her.

Celia Rosenberg tosses and turns in her cold bed, reliving those moments of love and horror between Karl-Heinz Hausen and her. Her body feels again the pain and pleasure of her lover's hard penis driving into her more and more forcefully. She is suffocating beneath Karl-Heinz Hausen's weight. Trussed up in her clothes, her movements hampered, she is beset by panic-stricken fear that she will no longer be able to escape from the love of this man who is taking her interminably, as he has taken her at other times in other places, whose images kaleidoscope in her mind at the speed of light. The orgasm building within her gradually banishes the past and brings her back, dazed, panting and wordless, to the present in that too bright room and the pain in her lower back which is pinned against a varnished wood chest of drawers on which Karl-Heinz Hausen has finally sat her to bring her once more to orgasm with his tongue.

The white cat leaps onto Celia Rosenberg's bed with an ear-splitting meow. Celia Rosenberg cries as she strokes her, still immersed in the memory of her ecstasy and the emptiness after Karl-Heinz Hausen's departure. She sees herself, huddled behind the screen, eyes closed to engrave on her memory the scent of the expensive perfume from Karl-Heinz Hausen's guests' furs.

Just then she hears a noise. She opens her eyes, holds her breath. An officer, his back turned, is taking his coat from the pile of clothes on the bed. He puts it on and, looking at himself in a cheval mirror, buttons it slowly. Hidden by the silk screen, Celia Rosenberg studies the officer. A very handsome man in his thirties with very blue eyes. He is tall with dark hair. He is putting on leather gloves. Celia Rosenberg recognizes the man Victor Hugo's spirit told her about through Gabrielle Lévy round a séance table, in Paris. "A tall man. You will know as soon as you see him. You knew him in a previous life, a long time ago."

Celia Rosenberg knows that this man was her father, in the past, in a very distant age. She wants to come out of her hiding place and throw herself, weeping, into his arms. The spirit had said, "You understand that, under no circumstances, must you speak to him." Celia Rosenberg had asked Gabrielle Lévy why this was forbidden. The Parisian replied that it was because of corridor 55. Celia had said that she didn't understand. The following Saturday, Gabrielle Lévy took her to her first meeting at Rabbi Kreutz's. Over the next few months Celia Rosenberg made stunning progress in her study of the cabala, much to the amazement of Gabrielle Lévy who had brought her there more or less by chance and had no idea to what extent Celia Rosenberg was destined for the cabalistic sciences.

Lying prostrate in the dark, her entire consciousness focused on the increasingly sharp pain in her chest, Celia Rosenberg trembles before the image of the green magician flickering in the glass of brandy Jacob Kreutz has handed her. Behind Jacob, she recognizes the Swiss woman, Marthe Thiers, who is as tall and lean as her own father is stocky and stout. There are others too from the resistance network whose names she forgets. Maie Deroine with bloodshot eyes one drunken evening at Chez Filou. Soshana Kreutz laughing till she cries in the cafe where they are in the habit of meeting after evenings studying the cabala. Soshana Kreutz and Gordon Thompson, a Canadian author whom they met in the Louvre and who sometimes invites them all to dinner in his small studio overlooking the Seine. Soshana Kreutz who said that the green magician was no more than a thought form that one could dissolve at will by creating a cone of energy above her. Beautiful, sad Soshana Kreutz, so sad, Celia Rosenberg remembers, so very sad.

Léopold Schwann is breathing heavily on her neck. She tries to extricate herself from his embrace. Beneath the chandelier in Sarah de Mouliak's reception room, Robert Desnos, his cheeks flushed bright red, winks suggestively at her. She wills him to come and save her from Léopold Schwann. Robert Desnos, looking very elegant in his tails, approaches and says to Celia Rosenberg as he holds his arm out to her, "Will you follow Rrose Sélavy to the country of decimal numbers where neither ruins nor evil exist?"

Something bursts in Celia Rosenberg's chest. Her heart is breaking, it seems as if her heart is breaking. In her distress she sees hundreds and hundreds of known and unknown faces pass before her at the speed of light. Klaus Schule, the musician seated at his piano is talking to her passionately about something which seems of the utmost importance but she is seeing again the men and women she knew in Paris stream past her. They all seem to want to talk to her at the same time about something she absolutely does not want to hear. Klaus Schule has stopped playing Erik Satie's *Trois Préludes pour le fils des étoiles*. Celia Rosenberg is moved to tears. Moved by the music and by the beauty of this man whose eyes shine like stars. She suddenly feels an irresistible desire for this man, such an intense desire that it wipes out all memory of Karl-Heinz Hausen. Klaus Schule has seen the desire in Celia Rosenberg's grey eyes. He talks about painting, about his birth in Dresden and his life in Munich, a career as a painter begun at the time of the *Der Blaue Reiter* movement and about how spirituality burst onto the art scene with Kandinsky, he talks about art and light, memory and stars. He is speaking so passionately that Celia Rosenberg forgets her desire for him and loses herself in the pictures crowding through her mind.

In her room in Brandenburg, Celia Rosenberg hugs the little cat to her aching heart. Celia Rosenberg did not realize at first that Klaus Schule was speaking to her in German and that she understood everything he was saying. It was only when Gracia Von Hendricks turned her head to see which of her compatriots was daring to speak in the language of the enemy in this fashionable evening packed with Jews and resistants that Celia Rosenberg realized that the words coming out of Klaus Schule's mouth were not French and that she, nevertheless, understood them. A blue horse gallops through the swirling ultramarine mists of her memory, travels through time, tramples on her heart.

Celia Rosenberg no longer knows whether it is the past or the future that has her heart in a vice-like grip as Klaus Schule bends to kiss her gently on the lips. His magenta blue eyes take her breath away and she becomes moist with desire for the musician who has knelt down and put his head on Celia Rosenberg's thighs as she trembles in her German bedroom at the memory of the man crying out as he came inside her.

Celia Rosenberg has finally dozed off for a few hours. In her dreams, Schnee, the little white cat is swimming in icy water and is then transformed into a blue fish gliding along a corridor of ice. In reality, the little animal is keeping watch, pupils dilated, ears pricked up. Who knows what she sees? Perhaps she is able to make out the shadow of the green magician who is pressing down with all her might on Celia Rosenberg's belly?

She wakes up, screaming. A ball of fire is raging through her womb. The pain in her chest has become so intense that she can hardly breathe; her screams are suffocating.

Frau Hausen, who has come running, sits her up against her pillows so that she can catch her breath. Celia Rosenberg is sweating profusely and, although she is shivering so much that her teeth are chattering, her skin is burning with fever. Everything becomes confused in Celia Rosenberg's mind. Gabrielle

Lévy is looking her straight in the eye and saying, "They even refused to give me milk at the dairy." Celia Rosenberg is running down the stairs from the sixth floor till she reaches the rue des Blancs-Manteaux where the psychic lives. She runs till she is out of breath along the rue des Archives to Jacques Coeur's house. The picture shifts to a damp cellar: a friar in a brown, hooded habit says his name is Fra Severino. Later, wielding a scalpel, he renders Jacques Coeur's right arm useless for the rest of his life. Celia Rosenberg moans and holds her right arm with her left hand while Frau Hausen tries to get her to drink a little water. "They even refused to give me milk at the dairy. They even refused to give me milk at the dairy." What if Gabrielle Lévy had been right? What if Gabrielle Lévy had been right about the rest too?

Celia Rosenberg thinks she will die of grief when her womb bursts and she finally understands that she is losing her child. Through her tears, in her delirium, she asks Frau Hausen if it is true that Hitler wants to eliminate the Jews. But the German woman does not understand French. Gabrielle Lévy looks up at Celia Rosenberg who is standing in her blue wool coat, ready to leave the tiny maid's room where the psychic practises her art and has just seen in her crystal ball dreadful danger connected to her relationship with the German officer. Celia Rosenberg is tying the belt around her blue wool coat when Gabrielle Lévy looks up at her and says, "They even refused to give me milk at the dairy."

Celia Rosenberg clings to Frau Hausen's forearm shouting unintelligibly. This goes on for a very long time. Several hours. In the early hours, Celia Rosenberg is bathed in her own blood and still shaking with fever, but she has survived. Patiently, Frau Hausen washes her, changes the sheets and forces her to drink a little hot soup. Then she takes Celia Rosenberg's hand, sits on the edge of the bed and tells her, in German, that yes, Hitler wants to eliminate the Jews. Celia Rosenberg doesn't understand what Frau Hausen is saying. A heavy, black wave of pain crashes over her heart. She moans, turns onto her stomach and sinks into a deep sleep.

Schnee is purring in Frau Hausen's lap. The pale, white morning sunlight filters into the bedroom where Celia Rosenberg is pacing interminably along iron corridors with the green magician at her heels. "They even refused to give me milk at the dairy." Gabrielle Lévy whispers to Celia Rosenberg who is looking for corridor 55. She finally finds it and starts running till she is out of breath and emerges on to an immense grassland in Louisiana; pink magnolias sway gently in the breeze. Karl-Heinz Hausen opens his arms to her. She rushes into them, he throws her to the ground and makes love to her under the magnolia tree, but a baby is crying somewhere and Celia Rosenberg tries to extricate herself from his embrace. That is her baby who is crying, her baby!

Over the following days, feverish and delirious, Celia Rosenberg relives the horror of Laurence's betrayal. Father Kelly tells her that it was Monsieur de Mouliak who denounced the resistance network. Gabrielle Lévy and Marthe Thiers have been taken away. Léopold Schwann is safely hidden in Amsterdam. Lola-Valérie, has refused to help them anymore. She is panic-stricken by the attitude of Laurence who has become downright racist since meeting the old aristocrat whose wife has barely managed to flee to Switzerland to escape his next denunciation. "Sarah, Sarah," Celia Rosenberg murmurs, cradling Schnee, the little white cat as it cries. "Sarah, Clara, Lola, where are you, my friends?" Celia Rosenberg whimpers as Frau Hausen makes her drink a little soup.

For weeks, for months, the green magician waits patiently, crouched in a corner of Celia Rosenberg's bedroom. For weeks, for months, the little white cat, cries, panic-stricken. For weeks, for months, in the dark tunnel of her dreamless nights, Celia Rosenberg hears Gabrielle Lévy repeating, "They even refused to give me milk at the dairy."

For weeks, for months, Celia Rosenberg lets herself slide into the fiery hands of death. For weeks, for months, Celia Rosenberg awaits the moment when Karl-Heinz Hausen will appear in the doorway of her bedroom in Brandenburg and carry her off to her enchanted Louisana. But, for weeks, for months, Karl-Heinz Hausen does not return. Celia Rosenberg thinks she is going mad with helplessness and sadness. Celia Rosenberg has never worn the yellow star. Celia Rosenberg does not want to understand what it means to wear the yellow star. Celia Rosenberg does not want to understand what it means to be Jewish and madly in love with a Nazi officer. She does not want to understand. For weeks, for months.

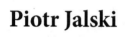

Piotr Jalski

The car drives slowly through the Polish countryside. She smoothes her black taffeta dress over her knees with her gloved hand. The warm morning breeze hums softly against the half-open window. August 6, 1944 will be Celia Rosenberg and Karl-Heinz Hausen's wedding day. She blinks as she promises herself to remember August 6, 1944, for the car has just rounded a bend and the glare of the sun is blinding her. Deep inside she sings softly, August 6, 1944.

The car has stopped in front of what looks like a town hall. He has opened the car door, is holding his hand out to her. He says "Elsa?" as if to wake her from her daydream. She gives him a reproachful look. She doesn't like him calling her "Elsa." Even though that is the name on her papers: Elsa Lagueux. Nationality: French. Date of birth: September 22, 1920. Place of birth: Paris. She wonders why he has not changed her date of birth, holds out her gloved hand to him and gets out of the car.

He takes her arm to climb the steps where two rows of young German soldiers, all blonde, are standing to attention. She puts her hand up to her black straw hat which is threatening to blow away in the wind. The swastika flag floats against a blue sky. As she lowers her gaze to the steps, she has a strange feeling that she has already done this. Exactly this, down to the last detail. The blue sky, the swastika flag, the uniformly blonde young German soldiers, the hot wind trying to tear her hat off her head. Then, just as she tightens her grip on her lover's arm to enter the building, the impression fades.

The hall is immense, harshly lit in spite of the daylight streaming through the high side windows. A dais, draped in red and hung with swastikas stands at the front of the hall. He leads her to the left, sits down in one of the rows. She copies him, obediently. He has taken off his cap and is mopping his forehead. His blonde hair is damp. "Yet it is not that hot," she thinks.

Several other couples are now seated. Monochrome women dressed in burgundy or brown dresses, hats and gloves. Polish women. And German officers. She thinks it is probably a group wedding. She looks at her lover. He is still mopping his forehead. He is tense, nervous. This surprises her. She doesn't really understand anymore. Nor does she really remember anymore.

The orator is speaking German. She doesn't understand German. She plays with her lace gloves. The man beside her is dreadfully nervous. Waves of white energy penetrate her heart. She raises her eyes to the speaker who is holding forth at the top of his voice. He is a tall, elegant SS. His hair is very black, his eyes blaze. He speaks violently, passionately. His deep voice is vibrant, hypnotic. She is surprised that she is trying to understand what he is talking about. A young Polish woman dressed entirely in white, and a young, golden-haired Nazi officer are seated at the head table. No doubt the bride and groom.

She closes her eyes. She is in Louisiana. She is spinning round in a white crinoline and a bride's veil, barefoot on an emerald lawn. He, in a white evening jacket, is laughing till he is out of breath. It is their wedding day. She is happy, perfectly happy. The sun warms her and she closes her eyes in pleasure as her husband blows gently on her neck.

A burst of applause in the hall arouses her from her daydream. He motions that it is time to applaud. She applauds. The speaker continues his speech. For a few minutes she is captivated by the expression of faith and conviction on the handsome SS's face. Concentric waves of white light surround him and radiate into the hall. She can feel herself hanging on to the man's voice although she does not understand the language. A wonderful feeling of peace fills her lungs, she breathes more and more deeply, more and more serenely.

She sinks into the darkness behind her closed eyes. She is walking in a temple which is plunged in darkness, a long time, a very long time ago. She is guiding herself with her hands along the damp stone wall. Her body immersed in iridescent peace, she creeps slowly towards the voice calling to her from the depths of her subconscious. She opens her eyes, suddenly. But the speaker is not looking at her. He seems to be speaking ever louder and with increasing passion. Throughout the hall men and women alike are spellbound. Only the man beside her seems impervious to the speaker's seductive power.

The SS has lowered his voice now, his tone almost confidential. He is speaking very fast, urgently, but intimately. Images from another time creep into the wavering white light around him, suddenly hiding him from her gaze. She is in the desert, in front of the Sphinx on top of which a yellow-robed high priest is stationed haranguing the crowd of slaves.

A burst of cheering in the hall jolts her out of her vision. The green magician has sat down at the head table. She shivers in horror. But the speaker's voice rises again caressing her skin and quieting her breath, dissolving the vision of the green woman who vanishes in a puff of smoke. A spaceship has just landed at the African base. The man who gets out of it looks like a human being but is an *Atlanten*. He waves. She recognizes the speaker and is infinitely relieved.

Everything has happened as planned. It is all settled. The man beside her mops his forehead. The heat in the big, almost packed hall has become suffocating. The bride is obviously bored, the groom has a vacant air. She is trembling with happiness. A million years ago she had promised this Force to always recognize it. She recognizes it today. Her attention wavers in the pool of white energy and she leaves her body sitting on a chair in the big hall and rises into the air, floats through the ceiling, flows through the air above the building, above Poland, to remain suspended in the warm air of this August 6, 1944.

She feels again the movement of the train carrying her she

knows not where, far from Brandenburg from which she has fled during the night to go and find him in Poland. Frau Hausen said that he was in Poland. She doesn't know where in Poland, but she can't keep waiting and waiting and waiting for him. She jumps into a goods train and cries for hours, her arm wedged in the door to get a little air, exhausted and worried, horrified by Frau Hausen's revelations.

At night, through a narrow slit in the wagon's roof, she catches a glimpse of the Milky Way and eventually falls asleep lulled by the swaying of the train. When she wakes, the train has stopped. With great difficulty she opens the heavy wooden door, jumps onto the railway tracks. It is a beautiful spring day. Buds are bursting out on the trees, a dog is barking in the village. Three young soldiers are on watch on the small station platform. She approaches them. One of the trio notices her, whistles at her and elbows the other two who call out to her. She draws level with them and says, "I'm Jewish." The three young men burst out laughing. The boldest one puts his arm around her waist, whispers something in her ear. She repeats, "I'm Jewish." A new burst of laughter. Frau Hausen lied: it's not dangerous for Jews.

Later, she walks through the village and along a narrow road to an inn at the entrance to the next village. The innkeeper, a thickset, heavy featured, half deaf man, serves her a dark-fleshed fish that she barely touches.

The speaker, in a lyrical outburst, has just pronounced the word *schnee* and a little white cat claws at her memory as she runs through the Warsaw ghetto till she is gasping for breath. She sees herself in a cellar full of rabbis and old women crying and clasping small children to their breasts. She collapses onto a pile of coats in a corner, dazed by a vision of white arcades disappearing into the mists of time while Gabrielle Lévy whispers, "They even refused to give me milk at the dairy." She is running till she is out of breath between the narrow walls of Corridor 55 like she ran on the rue des Archives a few centuries before, to flee the memory, escape from that strange woman who can read her like an open book and who calls her Jacques Coeur, as if it were her name.

She opens her eyes, finds herself back in the glaring light of the big hall. She feels completely fulfilled. The Force has come back to earth. As in each life. Her memories unwind joyfully like a long white ribbon in the blue sky above the grey stone building. She is running till she is out of breath at night along a street in the Warsaw ghetto. Bombs are exploding practically everywhere, tall red geysers. She is desperately looking for shelter. Desperately. She is weak, very weak. She has eaten nothing since the dark-fleshed fish that the German innkeeper gave her. She has eaten nothing but she has walked and run, walked and run, crossed fields, villages, towns, rivers, invulnerable, frantic with love and pain, led across the German countryside by her absolute conviction about her destiny, slipping into empty goods wagons during the night and jumping from them while the train was still moving but slowing down as it approached towns. In Poland, she saw peasants gathered around a fire, roasting potatoes and, attracted by the smell, she almost begged them to share their meagre meal with her. But, as soon as she took a step towards them, fear wrapped itself around her like a tightly stretched skin about to snap. Fear had been stronger than hunger and had taken her to Warsaw where she is now running through the bombs looking for shelter. In a single leap she hurls herself into a stone stairway leading to a cellar, but a piece of shrapnel hits her right leg. She loses consciousness, sinks into the dark, murky peace of a primeval fear of death so dense that she glimpses the black light shining on the other side of the world.

The speaker is talking about the black light. She no longer recognizes the language, cannot break down the words. But she knows that the speaker is talking about the black light she saw on that night, in Warsaw, as her leg made her scream with pain and brought her back to reality. She remembers other red geysers, other explosions, a pursuit in the street, then hands, many hands grabbing her, examining her, dragging her towards the cellar and carrying her through the darkness where not a single light burns, a breathless blackness where breathing is suspended by the animal fear of not surviving. She remembers slipping again, appallingly slowly, into the milky-starred spiral of the nebula, drifting on waves of magnetic heat into complete oblivion at the end of the galaxy.

The man is perspiring more and more profusely and cracking his knuckles. She moves to take his hand, recreate the radiant fusion of their bodies so used to ecstasy. But he gives her such a furious look that her blood runs cold. She is screaming with pain in the cellar in the Warsaw ghetto; a gloved hand covers her mouth to stifle the cry, almost suffocating her. She sinks into the tunnel.

When she opens her eyes again in the hall hung with swastika decorated banners, the speaker is looking at her. He is still speaking, in German, she recognizes the words and sounds of German. She finally acknowledges that she understands German as the speaker fixes his gaze on her for a few seconds, long enough for him to indicate that he too has recognized her. An iridescent peace rises through her limbs, flows up her spine and surges into her head.

"Remember, Celia Rosenberg," the voice inside her head says. And she remembers someone examining her painful leg in the dark of a Warsaw cellar. A young man. He bandaged her leg in the dark. Massaged her back and shoulders in the dark of that cellar. So that she fell asleep peacefully, forgetting her leg, forgetting the pain.

That night in the cellar, she dreamt that she was dead and that Tutankhamen in person was mummifying her, enveloping her in strips of cloth to ensure her passage to immortality. That night in the cellar she heard, for the first time, in her dream, the voice saying, "Remember, Celia Rosenberg," like now, as the speaker gesticulates, passionately evoking "Die Heimat". A tear falls on Celia Rosenberg's cheek as she remembers another country, far, far away, beyond the frontiers of time. Once again, the Force reminds her of it.

The man beside her is becoming impatient at the length of

the speech. He seems to be the only one in the hall who is not mesmerized by the speaker. This surprises her. She has never understood this man. From the first day that they met in Paris, she has never understood this man. It's not just because he is German that he is strange. He is strange in his ability to hate so intensely that it makes him tremble, as does love.

The man beside her is indeed trembling from head to foot. He has stopped fighting the waves of white light, allows himself to be carried by them, is transfigured in a fraction of a second. "Remember, Celia Rosenberg," the voice repeats and the sun floods an inner courtyard where a few hens are pecking at the hard yellow earth in search of food. She looks up for she has recognized his footsteps. Francis of Assisi, his feet bare, a staff in his hand, smiles at her. Tonight, she will join him for life. She will have her long hair cut off, run away from the family home to take refuge in the Monastery of Saint Damian. She will learn to speak to the birds and live in God's light.

"Remember, Celia Rosenberg," the voice chants. She groans on the pallet they have laid for her in a corner of the cellar that has been transformed into a hospital. The medical student who bandaged her leg often strokes her upper and lower back and massages her neck to relieve the pain. But the wound becomes infected. The pain grows worse every day. She cries often as she looks through the basement window at the day breaking, night falling, German patrols passing, the few survivors going about their business. Several people have died in the cellars, some are still dying every day. They cannot bury them. So they pile them up in other cellars. They dig tunnels and put the bodies as far away as possible. But the smell of rotting human flesh penetrates the cellar more and more, creeps into their hair and clothes, sticks to their skin. A few cases of typhoid fever have broken out, the resistants begin to despair.

Then one day there is a general alert. A patrol has discovered the hiding place. She sees the medical student fall beneath the hail of bullets just a few metres from her pallet. The German checks that the Pole is well and truly dead, approaches her. She moans with fever and terror, curls up in a ball so as not to be hit in the heart with the bullet. The German raises her chin with his leather-gloved hand, looks into her eyes. It is the officer she glimpsed in the mirror in Berlin, in Karl-Heinz Hausen's house, the man who she thinks was her father in another life, beyond the frontiers of time. Dumbfounded, Celia Rosenberg, gazes into the eyes of this man who is looking for something in her eyes that he doesn't seem to find.

Then, in spite of the order passed on to her by Gabrielle Lévy, she speaks to the German, clutches his sleeve, and says, "Karl-Heinz Hausen?"

"Remember, Celia Rosenberg," the voice shouts. She opens her eyes, looks at the man trembling beside her. The people around them begin to notice, lose interest in the speaker to stare at the officer in his trance. Gently, very gently she takes the man's hand in hers, trying to bring him back to his usual state of consciousness.

There is a burst of applause. Kurt Hoechst approaches the dais to thank the speaker. He stands very erect like in front of the mirror in Berlin, like in the cellar in Warsaw where he took charge of her because she said his friend, Karl-Heinz Hausen's name, as if that name would save her life. He shakes the speaker's hand, grasps his right arm and raises it above his head to encourage the gathering to cheer once again.

She wholeheartedly applauds the SS officer who embodies the Force in this life. Bursts of black light fragment her vision as she claps her hands vigorously, much to the astonishment of the man beside her who is looking stubborn and bad-tempered again. Soon the black light has flooded her eyes to the point that, for a brief moment, she is completely blinded.

The blackness gradually dissipates over the next few hours. But not until she is gazing at a magnificent red sun setting over a field of wheat does she fully regain her sight. The wedding reception is in the country, at a farm. Three big tables covered with white tablecloths have been set up behind the stone farmhouse. The German officers are drinking together while the young Polish girls have gathered around the bride who is making them laugh with a story which seems to be hilariously funny. Celia Rosenberg, holding her straw hat in her hand, has moved away to watch the sunset. Karl-Heinz Hausen is talking to the bride's brother, a tow-haired, sickly young man who has immediately attracted his attention by asking if he is really Karl-Heinz Hausen, the egyptologist.

Celia Rosenberg runs a weary hand through her fine dark hair. The scent of ripe wheat and white cake hang in the afternoon air; the wind, rippling the ears of wheat and cooling her skin, feels good. The sun is a heavy red ball sinking into a sea of blood. Celia Rosenberg half turns and casts a glance in the direction of the guests. The bride, her blonde hair enhanced by the long pink ribbons floating round her face, is shaking her head emphatically. Her friends are now listening to her solemnly. It is the men's turn to roar with laughter. The grandmother keeps bringing out cakes, cream covered blinis and plates of steaming sausages which pile up on the festive tables.

Celia Rosenberg turns her back on the party, returns to the red sun which is slowly sinking. Already, the light has changed. The field of wheat ripples like a sea of shadows at her feet as the sky is set ablaze with red and blue glaciers that melt in the setting sun. Suddenly, a cold gust of wind makes her shiver. She feels a presence brush against her. The green magician begins running through the field of wheat, fleeing something that seems to terrify her. She is making straight for the blazing sphere, yapping like a jackal. Celia Rosenberg turns her head towards the wedding guests wondering if they can hear the magician. An impressive, well-built man of about forty is standing near her. She recognizes the bride's father, Piotr Jalski, to whom all the guests were introduced when they arrived. The farmer is wearing a blue jacket and brown trousers and seems extremely uncomfortable in his Sunday best. He doesn't say anything, simply gazes at her. His deep blue eyes burn with a distant fire. Celia Rosenberg turns slightly, surprising the green magician just as she disappears into the sun.

But an irresistible force makes her turn her head. Piotr Jalski is still watching her without saying a word. She casts a glance over her shoulder. Karl-Heinz Hausen and young Jalski are pacing back and forth, still talking animatedly. Someone has brought a radio into the yard and is trying to pick up a programme. Nobody seems to be paying attention to them. Celia Rosenberg turns to face the man directly, turning her back on the party. He smiles at her. The hot wind ruffles Celia Rosenberg's hair. She raises her hand to tidy a stray lock of hair, then stands still.

Bizarrely, the man copies her. She smiles. He smiles too. She closes her eyes. The scent of magnolias sweeps into her soul, delights her to the point that, eyes closed, she smiles again, while the red sun sinks gradually below the horizon. The man has also closed his eyes. She notices it when she opens hers. She says, in French, "My name is Elsa." He looks at her furiously. He knows she is lying, he knows. He knows she is Jewish. Jewish and blind. "So you don't know what's going on here?" his blue eyes, flashing with anger, ask. "You're blind, you're closing your eyes. You don't know anything?" Celia Rosenberg does not understand what this man, who both wants and hates her, means. She does not understand. She wants to go back to the others. She moves slightly. But Piotr Jalski has put his big hand on Celia Rosenberg's bare forearm. She freezes, as if electrified.

"Don't you recognize me?" the hand on her arm seems to say. The man, is looking at her, still silent, with such an alarmingly sad expression that she wants to flee as quickly as possible, find the others, return to the pleasure of the hot summer day that is coming to a peaceful close. "Don't you recognize me?" the eyes, suddenly lit by a final ray of the setting sun, also ask. Celia Rosenberg feels the ground split open beneath her feet and black pyramids embedded one inside the other, open up one after the other as she tries to get her breath back. Piotr Jalski has grasped her elbow. He is holding her firmly. Holding her firmly, snaring her in his eagle-like gaze. "Leave me alone," she exclaims, freeing her arm from the grasp of the farmer's large hand.

But she remains there, gazing at this man who desires and hates her with equal intensity. And as he watches her silently, pictures begin passing through Celia Rosenberg's mind. Hundreds of emaciated men, women and children, their heads shaved, are walking slowly, resigned and devastated, along a dusty road. Thousands of men, women and children drop with exhaustion, are trampled on by the others who are advancing inexorably, in a stupor. Swastikas and tanks merge with these grey images the horror of which make Celia Rosenberg shiver. She doesn't know where these images come from and becomes increasingly panic stricken.

Piotr Jalski continues sending her the pictures of what he has seen a few kilometres from his farm, images of German officers clicking their heels and shouting out orders, scenes of pits full to overflowing with corpses being covered with earth by mechanical shovels. Celia Rosenberg sees. Celia Rosenberg understands that she is blind and chooses not to see. She breaks away, runs to the tables in the courtyard, asks for a glass of champagne and hurriedly banishes the madman from her mind.

The champagne is undrinkable. The images pass before Celia Rosenberg's eyes, superimposing themselves on the party. Hundreds, thousands of men, women and children fall one after the other, simultaneously, into ever deeper pits. "They even refused to give me milk at the dairy," Gabrielle Lévy says.

Celia Rosenberg is back in Paris, four years earlier. Karl-Heinz Hausen has arranged to meet her at the Cercle Militaire. She is seated at a small round table covered with a tablecloth. She is smoking while she waits for him. She sees nothing, hears nothing, lost in her daydream. And then suddenly, that annoyingly insistent voice in her head repeats, "They even refused to give me milk at the dairy." The previous evening, Gabrielle Lévy said that, nowadays it was better not to be Jewish. That the Germans intended to eliminate the Jews from the surface of the earth. Celia Rosenberg bursts out laughing, alone at the little table in the Cercle Militaire. Two officers at the next table, turn towards her and are preparing to start up a conversation with her when Karl-Heinz Hausen suddenly appears carrying half a dozen roses. "Poor Gabrielle Lévy," Celia Rosenberg thinks, "poor woman she's losing her mind."

"Gabrielle Lévy died at Treblinka," a voice says. Celia Rosenberg turns round. Nobody. All the guests are gathered round the radio listening to a mazurka. Piotr Jalski is still standing near the field of wheat. Celia Rosenberg puts her glass of champagne down abruptly on the table, approaches the other guests. Young Jalski catches sight of her, gives her a look burning with desire. Karl-Heinz Hausen is deep in conversation with Kurt Hoechst; they are seated at the end of one of the tables, partly hidden by the group of people round the radio.

Celia Rosenberg takes young Jalski by the hand, looks towards the field of wheat to make absolutely sure that Piotr Jalski sees what she is up to and leads the young man into the big house. He plants a rough kiss on her lips, lifts up her skirt, and undoes one of her garters. Celia Rosenberg gestures to him to wait, steers him to a staircase which must lead to some bedrooms. The young man takes her into his room, throws her on his narrow bed, tears off her panties and takes her brutally from behind. Celia Rosenberg lets the young man, who is panting and labouring to maintain his erection, penetrate her at length. Supporting her head on her clenched fists, she thinks, "I'll have been unfaithful to Karl-Heinz Hausen on our very wedding day."

Marlene Dietrich's beautiful husky voice singing *Lili Marlene* rises from the courtyard. Some of the young women add their voices to their exiled compatriot's. Then Kurt Hoechst's outraged voice can be heard. He bellows an order, someone turns off the radio. There are a few embarrassed laughs. Celia Rosenberg is still letting young Jalski penetrate her. He is labouring more and more, sweating and moaning. The door opens.

Piotr Jalski is standing in the doorway watching them. Celia Rosenberg closes her eyes in shame. The young man, looking pathetic, closes his fly, straightens himself up. Piotr Jalski stands aside to let him leave. He closes the door, sits down on the narrow bed where Celia Rosenberg is still lying, eyes closed on her humiliation and anger. Piotr Jalski very gently strokes her hair, her forehead, her eyebrows, eyelids, nose, cheeks and the outline of her mouth. A tear runs down her cheek. He smoothes it with his finger.

Then he gets up, leaves the room and closes the door. Celia Rosenberg remains lying in the little room as darkness gradually creeps over it. She finally falls asleep. In her dream Gabrielle Lévy is falling endlessly into a pit while the green magician shrieks with joy above the abyss. When she wakes up, Celia Rosenberg realizes that it is now night. A ray of moonlight bathes the narrow bed on which she has curled up. All is quiet. The party must have finished quite some time ago. She hears footsteps on the stairs. Piotr Jalski, followed by Karl-Heinz Hausen, enters the room. Karl-Heinz Hausen helps her put on the snakeskin shoes she had dropped at the foot of the bed. He pulls her up quite roughly by the hand while the Pole closes the window, for it is chilly on this early August night.

That night, Celia Rosenberg hesitates for a long time. Karl-Heinz Hausen, has not fallen asleep after making love. He smokes one cigarette after another. Celia Rosenberg hesitates. When Kurt Hoechst brought her, sick and exhausted, to him in Warsaw, Karl-Heinz Hausen, dumbfounded at finding the woman he loves above all else, braving Nazi Germany to find him and surviving, particularly that, surviving in such conditions, made her swear for her safety and his to never, absolutely never ask questions. Celia Rosenberg promised. And since then, she has never asked a single question.

Nevertheless that night, Celia Rosenberg hesitates. She too smokes a great many cigarettes. She watches her lover's profile outlined on the wall of their bedroom, dimly lit by the moon. She sees him again on their date at the Cercle Militaire where he has brought her red roses which smell of sweetness and desire like his skin, that of a well nourished blonde. She sees that night spent waiting for him, seated at the little table at the Cercle

Militaire, looking at and smelling the roses he has given her, wondering what Gabrielle Lévy wants to awaken in her with her never-ending suspicions. She sees herself, worried nevertheless, waiting for him all night seated at that table. For no sooner had he sat down beside her, than a messenger arrived with an urgent dispatch for him, so that he had to leave for an hour or two. Celia Rosenberg decided to wait for him there. She waited all night. All night spent desiring him, dreaming of the Louisiana where they planned to go together, after the war. All night hearing that intrusive voice repeating, "They even refused to give me milk at the dairy," with its thousand and one hidden meanings.

She remembers Paris, the rue des Blancs-Manteaux, Gabrielle Lévy's little maid's room, her séance table and Victor Hugo's spirit saying that black light is at the heart of human sentiment. An inner voice reminds her, "Remember, Celia Rosenberg." At that moment Celia Rosenberg breaks the seal of silence between Karl-Heinz Hausen and her. She asks, "Treblinka, do you know what it is?"

Very slowly, Karl-Heinz Hausen stubs out his cigarette. He gets up, dresses in the dark, leaves the room. Celia Rosenberg hears him waking the chauffeur and leaving the house they have only been living in for a short time and which she cannot get used to. Celia Rosenberg is now all alone in the big, deserted house. Suddenly, fear takes hold of her, her throat constricts like a frightened animal's. The fear is so strong that she moans and writhes for a few minutes. Then she calms down. Celia Rosenberg rolls onto her side to see more clearly the first light of day gradually filtering through the window overlooking the park and the street. She no longer knows what is happening. Everything is grey: the dawn, the light in the bedroom. Shadowy masses flow through the half-light, masses of cold, grey air, masses heavy with emotion, charged with electricity. But Celia Rosenberg, feels nothing. She lies prostrate, waiting. She is waiting for the end, as she does every time. She knows, as she always does. A sort of intense emptiness floods every pore of her body, seeps into her lungs, her soul. Celia Rosenberg bathes in the endless grey of her sorrow. "Julian," she moans, then immediately stifles the obscene memory of her early life.

Towards nine thirty in the morning, the heavy *traction avant* comes up the driveway. A few minutes later, Karl-Heinz Hausen, freshly shaved, wearing boots gloves and cap, impeccable in his black SS uniform, bursts into the room with Kurt Hoechst and another officer whom she has never seen. Karl-Heinz Hausen tells her to follow them and to look sharp about it.

Celia Rosenberg, does not move a muscle. She dares not appear nude before the two officers. Karl-Heinz Hausen throws back the duvet and the sheet, uncovering her completely. She gets up, slips into the previous evening's taffeta dress and puts on her snakeskin shoes without bothering to put on stockings and underwear, grabs her hat and follows on the heels of Karl-Heinz Hausen and the two officers.

They drive along the Vistula river for a long time. The sun finally clears the light morning mist. The youngest officer is driving. Kurt Hoechst is sitting in the front, smoking silently. Karl-Heinz Hausen, seated beside Celia Rosenberg on the back seat, has retreated into silence.

The wind ruffles the ripe wheat. Celia Rosenberg would like to breathe the fresh air but all the windows are closed and she certainly does not dare ask them to open them. The lack of air bothers her to the point that she is afraid she will have a dizzy spell. She turns towards Karl-Heinz Hausen and catches sight, very clearly, of the figure of the diabolical magician, in his green eyes. But he quickly turns his head away to gaze at the countryside.

On the banks of the Vistula, a pair of swans, feathers ruffled, are tearing each other apart, pecking aggressively, in a tragic, silent ballet. One of them has been wounded in the neck and spatters of blood are appearing on its white plumage. Celia Rosenberg averts her gaze.

Auschwitz

Auschwitz, August 7, 1944. Celia Rosenberg, flanked by Karl-Heinz Hausen and Kurt Hoechst, crosses a big empty room. The sun floods into the far end of the room skims over the long, dirt-darkened wood tables. A woman in uniform, stationed at the entrance to the brightly sunlit interior courtyard, watches them approach. "Heil Hitler," she shouts, clicking her heels and looking Karl-Heinz Hausen straight in the eyes with undisguised admiration. This surprises Celia Rosenberg more than everything else.

She precedes them towards a group of buildings on the other side of the narrow courtyard in the middle of which a gallows is set up. Celia Rosenberg sees a few tufts of grass that have managed to grow between the grey flagstones. The sun is hot, pleasantly hot on her bare arms. The sunlight makes Celia Rosenberg blink. Karl-Heinz Hausen stands on her right, erect and silent, Kurt Hoechst, on her left, is shining the toe of his boots with a cloth he has taken out of his pocket. Nothing happens for several long minutes.

Celia Rosenberg remembers being dead several times already. She is not afraid of death. She remembers the feeling of relief each time, and, each time, the anger at having forgotten everything or almost everything. She thinks, "This time, I will remember Celia Rosenberg. This time I will not forget." Karl-Heinz Hausen has turned towards the hut into which the woman in uniform has disappeared. He is becoming impatient. Celia Rosenberg looks into his green eyes which are ablaze with anger. She gives him a scornful smile. Does he really think he is frightening her? Celia Rosenberg is not afraid of death. She looks up at the gallows where a movement has attracted her attention. The green magician, her legs dangling in space, is sitting on the gallows, grinning maliciously. Celia Rosenberg takes a deep breath. A vaguely nauseating smell hangs in the air. "It's the smell of death," Celia Rosenberg thinks. "It's the smell of death."

The woman in uniform returns, accompanied by two soldiers flanking Piotr Jalski who closes his eyes against the dazzling sunshine. He is having difficulty walking because his legs are in chains and his hands are tied behind his back. He is still wearing the blue jacket, brown trousers and white shirt he was wearing the previous night. But the front of the shirt is torn open and he is no longer wearing a tie. The soldiers take him to the gallows and tie a rope around his neck.

Karl-Heinz Hausen has drawn close to Celia Rosenberg. He says, "Watch." Celia Rosenberg turns towards Karl-Heinz Hausen. He is drunk with hate. He signals to her to look at the gallows, shouts an order to the soldier who is closest to the Pole. Celia Rosenberg directs her gaze towards the gallows. Piotr Jalski is looking at her. His incredibly blue eyes radiate light. Celia Rosenberg averts her gaze.

Karl-Heinz Hausen grasps her chin and forces her to look at the Pole. Time seems to stand still. Celia Rosenberg gazes deep into Piotr Jalski's eyes. The man knows he is going to die. You can see it in his eyes, death is already there. Celia Rosenberg is ready to meet her own death. But not his. She lowers her eyes, moans. Tears run down her cheeks. Karl-Heinz Hausen forces her to raise her head. Piotr Jalski is looking at her with such sweet soulfulness that she cannot stop herself from crying. The Pole's eyes seem to be telling her, "Take heart. You're stronger than this, Celia Rosenberg," and she is suddenly ashamed of her tears. Images of thousands of men women and children, exhausted, almost beyond starvation, walking in silence, heads bowed, pass before her eyes. Celia Rosenberg raises her head, wipes away her tears. Piotr Jalski smiles while the soldier, at an order from Karl-Heinz Hausen, adjusts the noose around his neck.

Celia Rosenberg sees Piotr Jalski at the moment he entered his son's small bedroom for the second time that night. The magician in Celia Rosenberg's dream is laughing, her green lips curled in a sneer. Then the door opens. It is Piotr Jalski. He comes and sits on the bed beside her, strokes her face and hair again, asks,

"Were you sleeping?"

"I was dreaming. You speak French?"

"I speak Polish, German, Russian and French."

"What did you say to my husband?"

"Nothing. I had nothing to say to him."

"You didn't tell him that your son and I..."

"No, there was nothing to be said."

"So why did you follow us?"

"We've already met."

"Really? I don't remember."

"In Paris, in December 1941. Rue des Blancs-Manteaux."

"At Gabrielle Lévy's."

"Yes, at Gabrielle Lévy's."

"I don't remember."

"Gabrielle Lévy was very fond of you."

"Yes, I know."

"She died, at Treblinka."

"Treblinka, where's that?"

"Near Warsaw."

"How do you know she's dead?"

"We have friends in common."

"I don't remember meeting you at her place."

"But I remember."

"Did she do a séance?"

"No. We had more important things to do."

"What?"

"Are you that blind, Celia Rosenberg?"

"You remember my name..."

"I've never forgotten you."

"Why were you in Paris?"

"For the Resistance. Do you remember Rabbi Kreutz, Jacob and Soshanah Kreutz and Marthe Thiers?"

"Yes, of course."

"Marthe Thiers was responsible for helping the members of the network who were in the most danger escape to Switzerland."

"What about you, what did you do?"

"I helped several of my fellow countrymen escape from the Auschwitz death camp."

"Auschwitz?"

"You've never heard that word?"

"No."

"Nevertheless, your husband holds a very important position at Auschwitz."

Karl-Heinz Hausen bellows an order. With a loud snap the rope tightens and Piotr Jalski dangles in space, eyes wide open, still alive, although the noose is strangling him. Celia Rosenberg closes her eyes.

Piotr Jalski has stopped talking now. It is beginning to get dark in the bedroom. The guests are singing a Polish song at the top of their voices. Piotr Jalski is gazing at Celia Rosenberg. She raises herself on the pillow, brings her face close to the Pole's, kisses him gently on the lips. He returns the kiss, puts his arm around her waist, pulls her to him. Celia Rosenberg slips her hand under the white shirt, strokes the man's chest, presses her hand to his heart which is beating very fast, scratches his shoulders and neck, pulls him down beside her on the bed. Piotr Jalski turns the gaze of his blue eyes on her, their colour fading in the shadows. She looks him in the eyes for a long time. He says, "Your husband will kill me."

Celia Rosenberg stifles a cry, turns towards Karl-Heinz Hausen. She no longer sees any light in the SS officer's eyes. His eyes have become like a stormy sky, dark and lifeless. He is looking at her without seeing her, without hearing her. Celia Rosenberg grabs the sleeve of his uniform, shakes it, cries, "Karl-Heinz Hausen, Karl-Heinz Hausen." But Karl-Heinz Hausen neither sees nor hears her. He is watching the Pole, who, dangling at the end of the rope, is still breathing weakly as his face turns more and more purple.

Celia Rosenberg understands then that she has to choose. A vague flicker of light is barely visible in the depths of Karl-Heinz Hausen's eyes. She directs her gaze towards the man dying at the end of a rope, the man, who, although she has loved him only once, exudes love, love itself, the love she has been looking for since she was born.

She sees again the light in Piotr Jalski's eyes at the moment when he finally enters her, so slowly, so gently, that she trembles from head to foot. She sees again those eyes that say, "I love you," as the man moves to and fro within her, with a force and heat she has never known before, with such sincerity in his pleasure that she holds nothing back as she opens and gives herself, losing herself in those blue eyes that say that happiness is possible, yes possible, joy is possible, love is possible. She closes her eyes to better smell the sweet scent of magnolias but she is greeted by an impression of the sea, the impression of being an ocean within the ocean of his blue eyes, the eyes of the man who is now cradling her against him and saying, "I love you."

He strokes her naked back. She has taken off her dress to feel his body against hers, really feel the body of this man who is teaching her that she knows nothing, nothing at all about what is happening in Germany, Poland or Russia. Nothing.

"And you survived. It's incredible."

"That I survived?"

"Yes. No doubt your blindness has protected you."

"My blindness?"

"Do you know what your husband does?"

"No. I don't."

"He dismantles resistance networks, traps people in their homes, abducts their daughters, loots and burns their houses."

"And he leaves you alone?"

"For the moment. After all, my daughter, Olga, is marrying his friend Karl-Heinz Schulz."

"Does he know about your activities?"

"Yes, he is perfectly aware of them. But we have our strategies."

"Your daughter?"

"No. Olga doesn't know anything."

"Why?"

"It's better that way."

"Gabrielle Lévy used to say that sometimes it's better not to know."

"She died in the gas chamber at Treblinka."

"The gas chamber?"

"Of course, you don't know. But it doesn't matter now. The end is here. The Allies landed in June. The war will end soon. The horror is almost over."

"How can you be so sure?"

"We have allies in the next world. All those who are already dead."

"Gabrielle Lévy?"

"Yes, her, among others. It was undoubtedly she who brought you to me."

"You believe that?"

"Yes, I do."

Piotr Jalski is still alive. His skin is turning blue from lack of oxygen. Flashes of rage suddenly light up his eyes. "He doesn't want to die," Celia Rosenberg thinks, "he refuses to die." Celia Rosenberg catches sight of the green magician sitting on Piotr Jalski's shoulders, strangling him with her legs. Celia Rosenberg remembers Soshana Kreutz telling her about the cone of energy that you can visualise above the magician to make her disappear. She pictures a cone of energy and the witch immediately shatters into a million sparks of pure green light. Piotr Jalski is looking reproachfully at Celia Rosenberg. Does he believe she denounced him? Celia Rosenberg is torn apart by grief and doubt.

They are in the bedroom upstairs. The drunken guests are singing at the top of their voices. She is smoking a cigarette. Piotr Jalski is not smoking. A tree is casting strange, shadowy scenes on the wall.

"When the war is over, I'm going to live in Louisiana."

"Why Louisiana?"

"They speak French there. And because of the magnolias."

"You like magnolias?"

"I love magnolias more than anything else."

"You're different from the Celia Rosenberg I imagined."

"Different?"

"Gabrielle Lévy told me that you like the act of love more than anything else."

"Are you angry with me for making love with your son?"

"I don't understand."

"I saw that he wanted me without loving me. I prefer it like that."

"And with your husband?"

"Karl-Heinz Hausen doesn't know love."

"But you love him?"

"Yes, I love him."

Suddenly, Piotr Jalski, overcome by uncontrollable rage, puts his big hands round Celia Rosenberg's neck and squeezes, suffocating her. Then, just as suddenly, his anger subsides and he begins nibbling the neck he has just been brutalizing. He takes her again, violently this time, swearing under his breath, Polish swear words that Celia Rosenberg does not understand, but she knows that they are about women, who are all whores. But Celia Rosenberg feels Piotr Jalski's heart beating against her breast. And his heartbeat lulls her, sweeping her into all encompassing darkness that pulses with the love that reaches to the depth of their beings.

The green magician shows her black gums and bloody mouth just as the first waves of her orgasm begin to rise in Celia Rosenberg's trembling body. Fear robs her of her breath but the man, suddenly whispers in her ear, "Celia, Celia Rosenberg," and the magician disappears behind a heavy black velvet curtain. The rain is lashing down. Paris, October 1941, at Sarah de Mouliak's. Gabrielle Lévy says, "It's astonishing how much you look like your brother, Julian. I think I knew you both in another life, in Egypt." The rain is lashing down behind the heavy black velvet curtains. Now Piotr Jalski is massaging Celia Rosenberg's heart as she gasps for breath. Then he kisses her breasts gently, lingeringly.

"It's true, I like physical love more than anything. It's only in that intimacy with another body that I have the courage to re-examine everything that is filed away in my mind. I need to feel a heart beating against mine to confront the mental labyrinth. Gabrielle Lévy said that I had the gift. I've never understood what she meant by that. All I know is that my mind is haunted by images. That sometimes these images suffocate me. Gabrielle Lévy said I had to find corridor 55."

" Corridor 55?"

"I don't know what it is. Something like a rite of passage, I believe."

"It's the codename we used for the escape routes into Switzerland."

"Oh, I didn't know. But I'm sure there is also a cabalistic interpretation!"

"Gabrielle Lévy talked to me about you that time we met at her place. She talked about how blindly you loved that German officer who is now your husband."

"He's not my husband."

"I thought he was."

"No. Not really"

"Gabrielle Lévy spoke to you about Monsieur Kejec in the dairy, who refused to serve her any more."

" 'They even refused to give me milk at the dairy.' How do you remember the name of the man in her dairy?"

"Georges Kejec belonged to the network but, for security reasons, Gabrielle Lévy didn't know that yet. He had received orders to refuse to serve Jews to avoid suspicion. She had tried to warn you but you obviously paid no attention to what she said. You hardly looked at me the whole time we were there. You had come for a consultation for your friend Robert Desnos who wanted to contact Victor Hugo's spirit through her."

"But that's incredible! How did you come to remember Robert's name too?"

"It was the first time I heard his name. But I knew him very well later."

"You knew Robert Desnos?"

"Yes. I was very fond of him too. I haven't known where he is for several months."

At the memory of her friend Robert, whose puns always delighted her, Celia Rosenberg bursts into tears. Piotr Jalski strokes her hair.

"How could you leave everything, your life in Paris, your friends, to follow that Nazi who doesn't love you to Germany?"

"I swore to be faithful to him in another life."

"In another life?"

"Yes, in Canada in the 18th century. I was a naive, wholesome, country girl pregnant by an Indian. I was madly in love with him. Madly in love with the child I was carrying. When it was born, my father, who was old and full of hatred, seized the child and turned me out of the family home. I worked for a long time as a tavern-keeper at the Chien d'Or in Québec. It was a big cabaret frequented by soldiers and couriers. That's where I met a lieutenant in the infantry who was my lover and with whom I tried in vain to have a child. Then I began eating and eating so as to feel again the big belly I had loved, the child I had carried with so much love. Finally they shut me up in an asylum where I spent twenty years dreaming about seeing again the only child that had come out of my womb and that I had not even been able to hold in my arms for a single moment. I was called Rose-Mélanie Boulanger."

"How can you remember all that?"

"I just remember."

"And your husband is that child?"

"Yes. I didn't know immediately. But I carried a child of his in Germany. I lost the child. That was when I remembered that life in Canada."

"And that's why you followed him to Germany. The man who was the enemy of your people?"

"He was also Francis of Assisi in another life."

"That day, after you left wearing your blue wool coat and blue shoes in which your feet must have been freezing, Gabrielle Lévy told me about you and me in another life too."

"What did she say?"

"She'd noticed that I was troubled. She told me I had tortured you in the Middle Ages when we were both companions of Saint James and that you weren't about to forget it."

"I was a man then?"

"Yes, you were a man. That's what she said."

"Yes, I know. It's true that you still frighten me, Fra Severino. I remember being Jacques Coeur. But I'm ready to forget. Yes, now. Make love to me again, Piotr Jalski."

"Gabrielle Lévy also said that we were two stars in the sky. That it might take some time but we would end up meeting."

Piotr Jalski is now barely breathing. His gaze comes to rest on the toes of Celia Rosenberg's snakeskin shoes, on Kurt Hoechst's boots, lingers on the blades of grass growing between the paving stones, the patch of blue sky standing out above the cluster of huts. Then he looks at Karl-Heinz Hausen. And at Celia Rosenberg again. As if he were trying to take the memory of this last moment of life with him into death.

"I haven't made love for a long time."

"Did your wife die a long time ago?"

"Ten years ago."

"Did you love her?"

"I loved her."

"Did she look like Olga, your daughter?"

"No, not at all. Anna had dark hair, like you. Silky hair like a swan's feathers. She was Jewish too."

"So your daughter has Jewish blood?"

"Yes, in spite of her Russian name. I'm telling you things that I probably shouldn't tell you."

"Are you a Communist?"

"Of course I'm a Communist."

"Do they know?"

"Of course they know."

"I still don't understand why they leave you alone."

"They have their reasons, believe me."

"It's strange that nobody is worried about your or my absence."

"Your husband and the SS Gruppenführer Hoechst had to go back to Cracow for an emergency."

"But?"

"Your husband thought you were sleeping. He said he'd come back for you later in the evening."

"But he could come back at any minute!"

"I want you, Celia Rosenberg. I want to make love to your body, Celia Rosenberg. Your body is made for love."

"That's what my brother, Julian, said."

"Your brother?"

"Yes, my brother Julian. He was my first lover."

"Tell me about yourself, Celia Rosenberg."

"I was born in Mulhouse, in Alsace. I loved my brother Julian and hated my sister Esther. I shouldn't have hated her so much. She had tuberculosis. She was my father's daughter from a first marriage. She was twenty years older than me. She stayed shut up in her bedroom, crying and groaning all the time. I hated her so passionately. She's dead now. And I'm sorry I hated her so much."

"Why did you hate her?"

"I've never known why. Now I believe she was my father in that life in which my child was taken from me."

"Do you believe that's what happens, Celia Rosenberg? That we meet from one life to another to love and hate each other again and again?"

"I don't know. Make love to me, make me forget."

Celia Rosenberg is standing in that sunny courtyard before
the gallows on which a man is dying; she has known him for
only a few hours, but he means more to her than anything else
in the world. Tears of pain glisten in the dying Pole's blue eyes,
like when, as they made love, Celia Rosenberg, tipping her head
back and clinging to his arms, saw the reflections of the moon
dancing in his blue, night-darkened eyes. She has so much confidence in this solid, muscular body, this peasant's body which
merges so perfectly with hers that she abandons herself without
a sound, to silken, voluptuous ecstasy as if a blue angel with
downy wings were cradling her, carrying her off to heal her from
all the world's suffering which is dying in her panting body. Eyes
closed, Celia Rosenberg flies into the heart of the Milky Way,
held close in the arms of this man who knows better than she
the goodness of the galactic milk of life of which Hitler and his
acolytes are depriving their fellows a few kilometres from this
farm where they are making love, while Olga Jalski celebrates
her marriage to a black-uniformed SS from the Auschwitz concentration camp. Celia Rosenberg fights the nausea that takes
hold of her as she flies over heaps of corpses rolling through spiral nebula, decomposing, astral bodies, torn to pieces by the cosmic winds.

A vast magnetic light tears them from the Milky Way, sucks
them at an astounding speed towards the Cygnus constellation.
Piotr Jalski is still holding her in his embrace. Their luminous
bodies radiate energy and love as a ray of blue light surrounds
them and carries them from star to star till they reach Lambda
where they are expected.

"I dreamt that we were both dead."

"You were dreaming, Celia Rosenberg? While I was making
love to you?"

"Weren't you there with me among the stars?"

"It's possible. I've forgotten everything. Your neck is white,
so white and the skin is so delicate."

"I like it when you bite my neck, Piotr Jalski."

"I like it when you don't talk, Celia Rosenberg."

Piotr Jalski slides his erect penis into Celia Rosenberg's mouth. She places her hands on the man's thighs, sucks in the penis that is swollen with desire, runs her tongue round the foreskin. She abandons her body to the waves of bliss stirred up by the penis moving back and forth in her mouth. Her cheeks are burning, her eyes are burning. The man whispers, "Hamsa, little soul, Hamsa." He strokes her neck, the nape of her neck, her hair. Celia Rosenberg feels like an infant flooded with love and milk as the man comes in her mouth, a long warm flow that leaves her sated, dazzled, in love. "Hamsa, Hamsa, little soul," say the lips he is now pressing to hers as she sings a Jewish song she has not sung since she was a child.

"La la la, la la/La la la la, la la," Celia Rosenberg sings, holding her breath between phrases as her sister Esther taught her. "La la la, la la/La la la la, la la," Piotr Jalski picks up the refrain learning it from her lips. "Hamsa, little soul, Hamsa," Piotr Jalski says as he falls asleep. Her body pressed to his, Celia Rosenberg tries to enter his dreams with him. He smiles in his sleep, hugs her closer to him as they slip across the grass beneath a flowering magnolia tree.

When Celia Rosenberg opens her eyes, Piotr Jalski is kneeling between her thighs, his penis thrust into her, exploring her, shaking her to the depths of her being. Her breath comes faster, she raises her torso, floats on waves of joy beneath his embrace. The man has now put his hands on her back, pulls her towards him. Celia Rosenberg's womanhood is nothing but a fiery cave, a burning black hole in which she comes to orgasm releasing a stream of lava that floods her thighs and the man's, as he collapses on her stomach, hammering her cervix with his long, hot, hard penis, opening and taking her just as she feels she will die from pleasure.

Piotr Jalski is going to die. Standing beneath the blazing sun in the courtyard of the Auschwitz-Kasernenstrasse camp, Celia Rosenberg realizes that this man, whom she has loved for several hours with all her heart, is going to die at any moment. They seem to be separated by an eternity from the moment of total pleasure that united them. Another eternity opens up between the moment when she realizes he is going to die and the moment when that death will be irreversible, will belong to the past.

Lost in eternity, Celia Rosenberg turns towards Karl-Heinz Hausen. "My love," Celia Rosenberg thinks, "my love help me find my way." She reaches out her gloved hand to the SS officer's forearm, tries to find the heat of their union again. But Karl-Heinz Hausen throws her a sarcastic look. Celia Rosenberg glimpses, in the depths of Karl-Heinz Hausen's eyes, the black flame of a grief even greater than hers, greater than that of the Pole, than that of those men, women and children who are led to the slaughter house every day. Far away, in the depths of Karl-Heinz Hausen's eyes, far, very far away, a cold planet is turning slowly. "There is nothing human about this man," Celia Rosenberg thinks, backing away in horror.

Suddenly, Karl-Heinz Hausen seems like an android to her, a machine programmed to destroy, destroy and destroy until all life is exterminated. Howling terror resounds in Celia Rosenberg's mind. No, it can't be. That. The dark force, that subconscious magma, it cannot be. Karl-Heinz Hausen turns to look at her, his eyes like emeralds shining in the sun. Celia Rosenberg searches for a spark of humanity in those Aryan eyes, the spark of humanity one can sometimes see in a dog's eyes. But there is no remnant of humanity in his pure, immaculate blondeness outlined against the blue of the sky, in the eyes like pure water that nothing can disturb, these hard, bright eyes that reflect the light without absorbing it. "They're Hyperboreans from Thule," her cousin Gunther used to say. "They were the first inhabitants of the earth and want to become masters of the world again. They are made of ice, Celia, made of ice, I assure you." But Celia Rosenberg refused to listen to her cousin Gunther who dared talk about the Germans in front of Fritz, on the terrace of the café where he had told her about Gabrielle Lévy's role in the Resistance. Dumbfounded by her cousin's daring, Celia Rosenberg did not asked any questions about these astral entities which, according to Gunther, had reincarnated themselves to recreate their empire. Fritz appeared not to have heard. But Celia Rosenberg was never sure. Fritz disappeared the following day and was never seen again by Emmanuelle or anyone else.

"Was Fritz in the resistance?"

"Fritz Muller? Yes. How did you guess, Celia Rosenberg?"

"Have you ever heard of the Hyperboreans?"

"No. Who are they?"

"I don't know. It doesn't matter. Maybe you'd better go before my husband comes back, Piotr Jalski."

Celia Rosenberg finally averts her gaze from the green stones glittering in Karl-Heinz Hausen's eyes. Celia Rosenberg knows that she loves this man as she loves the scent of magnolias and the taste of milk. Celia Rosenberg knows that she loves this man more than she has ever loved any human being on earth. More than she loved her father and mother, more than she loved her sister, Esther and brother Julian. More than she loved Hans Meyer and Maurice Pons. More than she loved Sarah, Lola-Valérie, Clara la Brune, Klaus Schule, Maie Deroine or Léopold Schwann. Everyone she has known in her life passes before her eyes at the speed of light, and, although she knows that she loved them all, Gracia von Hendricks and Gabrielle Lévy, her cousin Pascal, her aunt Laure, her cousin Gunther, Frau Hausen, and that woman whom she had never seen again, Mariette Dupont, her blonde hair shining in the late afternoon sun on a Paris terrace in 1942, Celia Rosenberg knows that she has never loved anyone more intensely than she has loved Karl-Heinz Hausen.

This man is no longer human, this man whom she has loved with all her heart. He is a handsome, miserable machine in the grip of hysteria, standing erect, in front of her, his chin up, a look of pride in his eyes. "Karl-Heinz Hausen" Celia Rosenberg whimpers, unable to accept the truth, denying the glaring truth. This man is no longer human, Celia Rosenberg. He is a god, Celia Rosenberg, a cruel, merciless god, as cruel as his green eyes, as merciless as the black flame of his pupils. He is a superman playing at war, Celia Rosenberg, a being come from the dawn of time to incarnate death, to put death to work.

Celia Rosenberg bursts out laughing. Karl-Heinz Hausen gives a start, shouts an order. The woman in uniform approaches him, ready to receive his orders. But Karl-Heinz Hausen says nothing. Piotr Jalski looks at him, without anger, with a kind of curiosity tinged with goodness and suffering. Celia Rosenberg is watching Piotr Jalski, who now turns his gaze towards her. A white sun seems to burst in Celia Rosenberg's heart. She feels all the love in the world for this man who will soon die, all the love in the world. This is the man she wants to follow till the end of time, love till the end of time. This man, Piotr Jalski, his blue gaze fading little by little, barely sees the love beaming towards him at the moment life leaves him.

Piotr Jalski has closed his eyes. Piotr Jalski no longer exists. Celia Rosenberg has given him her soul, and he no longer exists. Piotr Jalski has set out on the paths of death, leaving Celia Rosenberg alone in the midst of machine-beings on a planet that they are in the process of debasing, crystallising in black light. Piotr Jalski is floating above the gallows, a black knight carrying his standard emblazoned with a white rose across the sky. He is galloping towards the sun, a black knight of the forces of light, while Celia Rosenberg, sees, through a veil of tears, the two SS and the woman in uniform slowly approaching her.

Then, she shouts. Celia Rosenberg shouts, with all the strength of her being. "Ich bin Jüden," an assertion of her identity in the very face of those who want to annihilate her. Karl-Heinz Hausen covers Celia Rosenberg's mouth violently with his leather gloved hand. She collapses. Crumples to the ground, gets up and starts running.

Celia Rosenberg runs through the empty room, overturns a bench, bumps into a prisoner who is washing the floor, emerges in front of the main building of Auschwitz-Kasernen-strasse, dashes towards the barbed wire fence, rushes towards a young soldier who points his bayonet at her. Let him run her through, let her die, let her die. A huge dog, barking at the top of its voice, jumps on her but the young soldier holds it back by its collar, stops it from biting Celia Rosenberg. Karl-Heinz

Hausen arrives at a run, covers Celia Rosenberg's mouth with his hand as she shouts, "Ich bin Jüden," so that they will finally finish her off, finish her off. So that she can join in death the man she now loves more than herself, till the end of time. But Karl-Heinz Hausen pulls on Celia Rosenberg's arm, drags her inside the building, shuts her in his office where she begins screaming, "Ich bin Jüden," throwing ashtrays, folders, a globe, everything she can get her hands on.

The Cygnus Constellation

I'm in the dark, my love. I'm trying to remember. I remember that, when I threw the little blue china hippopotamus which was on Karl-Heinz's desk and it shattered, my husband threw himself on me and hit me with a strength born of despair. It's difficult for me to picture the scene, my love. My whole body still aches from the blows. I knew how much he loved that statuette but I was mad with grief after your death, my love, mad with grief. As he was hitting me as hard as he could, carried away by rage, I saw, for one last time, love shining in the eyes of the man I had loved and who had loved me. I was sure of it as he was beating me. I saw that Karl-Heinz also, was mad with grief.

Then the woman whom he called "Brunehaut," as if he knew her intimately, entered. It was the woman in uniform who was at your hanging. Karl-Heinz begged her not to say anything. She was about forty, cold, with a hard look in her eyes. She quickly left the room, closing the door behind her. Karl-Heinz was staggering with fear. He saw me lying in a corner, covered in blood, and gave me a kick as if I were a burdensome animal. I lost consciousness.

I must have spent two, or maybe three days, in that darkness, my love. I can still taste my blood in my mouth. Nobody has come. There are two other women with me in the dark. One of them, the old one I believe, is crouching motionless in a corner. I can only hear her breath coming in gasps and I can feel her fear, like an octopus slithering in the dark. The other one is a very young girl, almost a child. She cries from time to time.

She calls for her mother. No one has brought us food or water since I regained consciousness.

I don't want to forget anything, my love. Nothing. I lick the blood on my lips to remind me of your kisses. I cry because I have already forgotten the taste of your mouth, my love. Where are you my love? Can you see me curled up in the dark, can you hear me? What have they done with your body, what became of your body since life was taken from it? But death is nothing, my love. Death is nothing: I will pass through death.

Will you forgive me for holding it against you when you confessed that it was you who denounced Gabrielle to prevent even more people being tortured by the Gestapo? Will you forgive me for thinking you were weak and cowardly then, as if you'd had the choice? Will you forgive me for suspecting you of collaborating with the Germans? Will you forgive that I could still not understand how you managed to return to Poland safe and sound after the raid that cost the lives of most of my friends? Will you forgive me one day, Piotr? Will you forgive me for having forgotten you during all those years, for forgetting our numinous meeting at the rue des Blancs-Manteaux?

Someone is crawling across the floor very close to me, hair brushes against me. It is the young girl. She is looking for a bit of warmth, curls up against me. I hug her, kiss her forehead. My ribs are hurting. The child is light, so light in my arms. She must be dying of hunger. I can feel her warm breath against my neck, hear her heart beating. I feel good, my love, strangely good as you watch over me and this trembling child from on high, over this woman who is now no more than a terror stricken bundle of rags.

Now the darkness is a soft cocoon, like the cradle of all existence as I slip into a blessed semblance of sleep with the child curled up trustingly against me like a little cat. Tears fill my eyes when I think of the living, my love. Death has us in its tight grasp and I am petrified by the sight of the snakes of a Medusa's head writhing in the green magician's viscous cauldron. But the child's warm hand dries my tears, strokes my face as she sings a

German lullaby. Such irony, my love, a German lullaby to put me to sleep in the German death that awaits me.

But I will pass through death, my love, I will pass through death. I will remember Celia Rosenberg and this little fourteen or fifteen-year-old girl cradling her in the dark. I will remember this. She and I in the mists of time. You and I in the mists of time, my love. This hunted woman who has more and more difficulty breathing in eternity. I will remember the ecstasy of this instant of eternity. You are dead, Piotr, yet I feel that you are alive. The child's heart is beating very fast, very fast as if to remind me of the living, my love.

I don't wish for death anymore, nevertheless it is coming; army boots on the cold paving. The door opens with a hellish creak. I cover my eyes which are already unaccustomed to light. Two officers take us into another hut. Several other women are there, heads shaved, dressed in a kind of grey sack like the one I too am wearing. A fat, red haired, big-busted woman shaves my and the young girl's heads. The child has beautiful, dark, sad eyes. She smiles at me as she bends her head to be shaved. The elegance of the movement makes me smile too. Another female guard bellows an order for us to get undressed. We take off our clothes.

Next, they make us form lines. The little dark-eyed girl manages to be beside me. I smile at her, as I think of you, my love whom I will join in death. I wonder if this child knows she is going to die. I think she knows. Her eyes are sad in spite of her smiles. No doubt, she would have liked to live. To live! To live! The wind carries the scent of pink magnolias to me, makes my heart leap with joy. To live! But we are walking slowly towards death, animals exhausted by suffering.

The young, dark-eyed girl takes my hand in hers, holds it to her heart, says, "Myriam." I reply, "Celia." We are walking towards the building that must be the one you called a gas chamber, my love. It is very early in the morning. The sun has hardly risen. We are naked, shivering. We are crammed into this cement building. They close the door. Myriam looks at me with the eyes of a hunted beast. I regret not having asked you to explain in more detail how these gas chambers work, my love. Suddenly I am afraid. I am afraid of suffering. I don't want to suffer, my love. I want to die and find you. Die and be set free, my love.

The green magician is running along a pipe on the ceiling, an astonishing speck of light in this room where thousands of us stand, distraught and terrified. I look at these naked men and women, the sad children, the tired, grey skins. A baby has begun to cry. Myriam's small hand clings tightly to mine. Her eyes tell me that she will never forget, that she will pass through death with me. I pull her small emaciated body to me and we cry like that, hugging each other as the gas begins to make the people around us cough. Several people begin screaming, some try to scramble over the bodies of the men and women who have already fallen in an attempt to live a few seconds longer. Then it is Myriam's turn to slip into death. I fall to the floor with her and keep her hand in mine. I am not yet dead when they come to open the doors.

The prisoners tasked with moving our bodies are wearing gas masks to carry us to the wagons. I didn't protest when they tore Myriam's hand from mine. I pretended to be dead. I'm pretending to be dead, my love, among these bodies being taken through the morning mist to the Birkenau ovens whose smell I recognize from your description of it. My feet are jammed against the metal of the wagon as it rolls along a bumpy railroad track. It's dreadfully painful. It's unbearable, my love, but that's how it is.

They finally unload us in front of the big crematorium ovens. I keep my eyes open so that I won't miss any of the blueness of the sky that manages to pierce through the thick, foul-smelling smoke. Someone drags me a short distance by the feet. My head bangs against stones. I have time to glimpse a strip of green grass dotted with bushes, the only splash of colour in this grey landscape.

Heavy, steely clouds are now rolling across the sky and fine drizzle begins falling, rapidly turning everything to mud. The man who was dragging me by the feet bends towards me to pick up my body and put it in the furnace. But, on seeing my eyes wide open, he drops me, terrified. His eyes are miraculously bright, yet he is so thin that I wonder from where he gathers the strength to drag me. His face is so filled with horror that I can't stop myself from closing my eyes to save him from even more suffering. He thought he was burning bodies. And they are bringing him ones that are still alive.

But the man shakes me, mumbling something I don't understand. I open my eyes again to see a toothless mouth trying in vain to say something to me. Klaus! This human wraith was the brilliant musician I knew and loved in Paris, a lifetime ago. Klaus! He has recognized me, drools words of hope and courage on my face. I see a blue horseman dancing in his eyes and I smile, my love, I smile one last time at life on this planet as he picks me up in his arms, holds me close. A kapo shouts, "Schnell," and gives him a blow on the head with his crop. The blue horseman gallops in a heavy wave of water in Klaus's eyes as, stunned, he loses his balance and falls backwards with my body in his arms. But he gets up immediately and carries me to the furnace where he crams me against three other bodies. I am still alive, my love, when Klaus closes the door of the crematorium oven.

I can feel still warm limbs around me and the terror permeating every cell in my body renders my breath irregular. I don't cry. I remember that I don't cry. I don't scream. I think about you. I remember thinking about you. I think about everything you told me on your daughter's wedding day. I think about the red sun setting above the field of wheat, the light in your eyes, the green magician with her legs dangling above the gallows. It is beginning to smell of burning flesh, my love. I'm suffocating. I'm coughing and spitting. The smell is so strong; what horror, my love what horror! The flames leap onto my back, it is burning. My back is on fire now and I am not able to think about you anymore, my love. I scream, I scream, I scream. Is it true that death is nothing, my love? Is it true that love is stronger than death?

I don't hurt any more now. I don't hurt any more but I'm even more afraid than before. I must be dead now, my love. I must be dead. I'm in the dark, my love. Where are you? I see something move beneath the thick smoke. It's the kapo beating Klaus with his crop. Klaus is lying in front of the furnace, his body racked with sobs. I can see Auschwitz-Kasernenstrasse at the end of the muddy track. The rain is lashing down. I can float at will, my love, float without even feeling the rain. Where are you, my love, where are you?

In Karl-Heinz's office, the woman in uniform whom he called Brunehaut, is busy putting away papers. Karl-Heinz comes into the office. It looks as if he has been drinking. The woman smiles at him. She tilts her head up with a seductive glint in her eyes. Karl-Heinz goes over to her, caresses her breasts, kisses her. I feel extremely jealous, which is strange, my love. Karl-Heinz takes her hastily on the divan in a corner of his office.

I catch sight of the buildings through the window. I fly over the courtyard where you were hung. Four gallows have now been set up. Three men and a woman are dying at the end of their ropes. Where are you my love? Where are you?

A convoy draws into the station. Hundreds of people fall from the wagons, walk with difficulty towards the officer who sorts them into groups. The rain is lashing down on Auschwitz, my love, and I'm searching this crowd of wretches knowing that you're not there. Where are you my love?

I can hear you, my love, I can hear you! I can feel you here, beside me. I can't see you. Only this train, the rain, the mud, the greyness. But I can feel you, my love, I can feel you. You say, "Remember, Celia Rosenberg," and immediately you are gone. Where are you my love? Where are you? I am sitting on the balcony of our house in Mulhouse, I am six years old. It is raining, it is summer. Hans Meyer has just moved to Hamburg. I am angry with the entire world. Mom offers me a glass of milk. I grab the glass out of her hands and throw it in her face. I go up to my room to cry. My sister, Esther, slaps me until I apologise. Mom is crying and tells her to leave me alone.

Tessa Meyer tells me that her brother died two years ago, in an aeroplane accident. I met her at Chez Filou. I am with Karl-Heinz, she is seated at the other table, with another German officer. She speaks to me in French. I wouldn't have believed she would remember French, after all these years.

I run to the Church of Saint Augustin, on boulevard Haussmann. I have never entered it before. I want to take refuge in this church which rings out the hours, forget my grief. But I bang my forehead against a carved wooden door which refuses to open. I only have a scarf on my head, it is cold. It is very cold.

Monsieur Nicolas is still wearing his bloodstained apron. Mom gives me a reproachful look. My cousin Gunther says that it is all just an illusion. This table, these people dining in Paris, on a summer evening, in 1942. He says, "Come Celia, I was Pharaoh Aknaton and you were part of my suite, don't you remember?" The scene fades slowly, as if the light were disappearing. Léopold smiles at me, his body disappears, all that remains is his smile. The green magician is sneering on the other side of the wall. There is a wall. I can feel that there is a wall. I'm afraid, my love, I'm afraid. I can no longer distinguish top from bottom, front from back. I'm disoriented, I'm afraid and I don't understand. Pictures are speeding past my eyes, pictures that keep changing, fading, returning to jump out in front of me. Colours swirl, merge, flow in every direction at once. I hear crackling, far away, somewhere far away. Closer now, a crackling sound. I remember that I must not resist the crackling; let the ice corridor close over me, melt through me, scatter me into a thousand of me, dancing and spinning tirelessly.

An angel of light has approached. He has the most beautiful smile I have ever seen, very long, curly blonde hair, rosy lips. He takes my hand and together we rise into the clouds. I see the Eiffel tower below me, my cousin Pascal waving to me. The angel has disappeared. It is a picture from my friend Catherine's catechism. I am six years old, it is Thursday. We are eating our afternoon snack. I have a doll with a blue dress called Christiane. Catherine shows me her catechism. It says that God is everywhere. She asks if we believe in God. I don't know. I say that I don't know. She gives me the picture of the angel to comfort me. I keep it in my copy of *Alice in Wonderland* for a long time. My sister Esther finds the picture and tears it up in front of me.

The angel is no longer there, my love, there's nothing there. Only water, water, water stretching to infinity. Only that memory of you, your blue-eyed gaze, just before you died.

Arbeit macht frei the sign above the barbed wire at the entrance to the Auschwitz camp says. *Arbeit macht frei*, my love: Work sets you free. I am tumbling through the tunnel of death, my love and these words haunt me. No! I will not be fooled, my love. Never again will words fool me; never again. Words are a dangerous trap in the mouths of madmen. *Arbeit macht frei*, my love: Hitler is putting us to death, us and millions like us, to turn us into cosmic slaves, cleanse the earth of undesirables and feed the astral plane with vengeful beings who will continue to obey him just as they blindly allowed themselves to be carried in cattle wagons towards death in the gas chambers and crematorium furnaces.

Arbeit macht frei, my love: *Arbeit macht frei*. Hitler is immortal, prince of the dark cosmos, alchemist of black light, the angel Lucifer of atomic fusion. *Arbeit macht frei*: perhaps work sets you free, but I don't want to be free at that price. I love life, my love. I am travelling through the narrow corridor of death and I love life, my love. I love watching big white swans glide across the clear waters of ponds, the perfect green of rivers, the deep blue of lakes like your blue eyes, my love. I love life and I refuse to be chained to death, I refuse to hate that ridiculous buffoon who believes he is stronger than life itself, because he is succeeding in killing us by the hundreds, by the thousands, by the millions. But we are immortal, my love, we are immortal. I die reminding myself of our immortality, I am dying of love of life while, already, my physical body no longer exists; my feelings and thoughts, light as air, carry me into the labyrinths of death in constellations of blue stars. I am dying of love because I am still alive, my love, everywhere on earth, in other bodies, in the bodies of the men and women who are still alive, and in other galaxies. *Arbeit macht frei*: work sets you free.

I see a blue horse galloping on the ocean's edge. Its nostrils wide, its lips curled back, its mane flying in the wind. Its hooves trample a wave of very, very blue, heavy water, you would say it is thick. It is galloping and galloping against the wind but is not making any progress. Nevertheless, it keeps galloping tirelessly. And then you are there, suddenly, on my neck. You have put your hands on my shoulders, your cheek against mine. You are looking at the hologram I have just drawn. You say that it is coming along well, very well. I am pleased. I am tired. I have worked all night. You bring me a glass of milk. Your skin is blue. Mine too. Our clothes are blue, too. Our house is made of glass, it is transparent. Outside, there is a desert. The sand is yellow, like on earth. You ask me if I remember the earth. Of course, I remember the earth, my love. Of course. That's what I wanted to portray with that frightened horse galloping and galloping but getting nowhere.

You burst out laughing. You say that, obviously, here, on Lambda in the Cygnus Constellation, horses are that colour. But you say that on earth horses are not blue. That my picture is not realistic. I say, "Don't you think so?" I drink my milk. I remember that on earth, I loved milk. "I think milk was white on earth?" You say yes, milk was white, my love.

I say that I remember that, as a child on earth, I dreamt about a big brown horse coming to wait for me in the morning, in front of my house, to go to school. I had a blue coat, a blue hood, brown leather gaiters. I mounted my horse and we trotted slowly to the school on roads that a light snow shower had covered during the night. The sky was yellow and very pale, over the town. I put down my glass of milk and say, "Shall I draw a brown horse now? What do you think?"

Yolande Villemaire is one of Quebec's most prolific writers, proficient in both poetry and prose. She has given poetry readings and performances around the world. She has lived in New York, Paris, Amsterdam, and India. Her novels have been translated in English and in Italian; her poetry has been translated in Spanish, Romanian, Catalan, Dutch, German, and Islandic. Her novel *La vie en prose* won an award from the *Journal de Montreal* in 1980 and her poems, *L'armoure* received a Radio-Canada award in 2002. She also received a Quebec-Mexico poetry prize in 2008 and the Career Award from Quebec's Council of Arts and Letters in 2009. Also in 2009, she was a guest of honor at the Festival de la Poésie de Montréal. She has published more than twenty-five books, four of which are available in English translation from Ekstasis Editions: *Midnight Tides of Amsterdam, Poets & Centaurs, India, India and Little Red Berries.* She has also published a book of poems written in English, *Silence Is a Healing Cave* (Ekstasis Editions, 2013). Yolande Villemaire lives in Montreal and is the director of TOTEMPOÉSIE.